A SAVAGE STATE
OF GRACE

By Donald MacKenzie

NOBODY HERE BY THAT NAME
RAVEN'S LONGEST NIGHT
RAVEN'S REVENGE
RAVEN AND THE PAPERHANGERS
RAVEN AFTER DARK
RAVEN SETTLES A SCORE
RAVEN AND THE KAMIKAZE
RAVEN AND THE RATCATCHER
RAVEN IN FLIGHT
THE SPREEWALD COLLECTION
ZALESKI'S PERCENTAGE
POSTSCRIPT TO A DEAD LETTER
SLEEP IS FOR THE RICH
THE KYLE CONTRACT
NIGHT BOAT FROM PUERTO VERDRA
DEAD STRAIGHT
THE QUIET KILLER
DEATH IS A FRIEND
SALUTE FROM A DEAD MAN
THE LONELY SIDE OF THE RIVER
COOL SLEEPS BALABAN
DOUBLE EXPOSURE
THE GENIAL STRANGER
KNIFE EDGE
DANGEROUS SILENCE
THE SCENT OF DANGER
THE JURYMAN
MAN HUNT
OCCUPATION THIEF

A SAVAGE STATE OF GRACE

DONALD MacKENZIE

PUBLISHED FOR THE CRIME CLUB BY
DOUBLEDAY
NEW YORK
1988

All of the characters in this book
are fictitious, and any resemblance
to actual persons, living or dead,
is purely coincidental.

Library of Congress Cataloging-in-Publication Data

MacKenzie, Donald, 1918–
A savage state of grace.

I. Title.
PR9199.3.M325S28   1988   813′.54   87-17112
ISBN 0-385-24317-0

BT 12.95/7.19-'88

For Hugh and Fozo with love

A SAVAGE STATE
OF GRACE

CHAPTER 1

It was late September in London and the atmosphere was stifling inside Knightsbridge Crown Court. Every unbarred window in the building was open. The jurors filed back into Court 1 and resumed their seats on the benches. By reaching out Raven could have touched both defendants. Neither of them looked at the other.

The man lounged in the dock in a well-cut blazer and hand-made loafers. A head of prematurely white hair and a deep sun-tan gave an air of raffish distinction to Piers Pelham. The girl sitting next to him was Helga Heumann, a twenty-two-year-old German with drab blond hair that was pinned up and skewered with a metal comb. She was wearing a black skirt and white nylon blouse. Fourteen weeks awaiting trial had given her a matt prison pallor.

The usher in charge of the jury, a ready source of courtroom gossip, said that the girl had had no visitors since her arrest. As far as Raven was concerned, Pelham's confident manner was likely to stem from the fact that Mark Culross Q.C. was his counsel. Culross had been a leading Treasury barrister who had switched to defence work. Since then, he had achieved a seventy per cent acquittal rate. The jury-room usher claimed that his fee for this trial was close to one hundred thousand pounds.

The Clerk of the Court rose, an Antiguan whose starched white bands accentuated the oatmeal color of her skin. She projected a voice made for a drum accompaniment.

"Have you been able to reach a unanimous verdict, members of the jury?"

The foreman looked beyond her to the grave-faced judge on the bench.

"No, Your Honour. And to be frank there doesn't seem much prospect of it."

He was Harvey Bullock, a produce-broker of Raven's age, dressed in a light summer suit.

Judge Salter's eyes were heavy-lidded. "You mean there is no likelihood at all, is that what you're saying?"

"I'm afraid there's a basic difference of opinion," said Bullock.

Raven stared straight ahead, ignoring the veiled accusation. The public galleries were crowded with onlookers, most of them regulars. They read books, dozed, did crossword puzzles, coming to life only when drama stirred. The two Drugs Squad officers in the case sat side by side near the witness-box.

Judge Salter consulted the gold half-hunter that lay open in front of him, and addressed the jury.

"What I'm going to ask you to do, ladies and gentlemen, is retire to your room again and make one last effort to reach a unanimous verdict. If that fails, I can accept a majority verdict of at least ten to two."

He indicated the jumble of exhibits on the table beneath him. Hotel registers, British Telecom records, and the heroin wrapped in heavy-gauge plastic.

"If there's anything there that you feel would help your deliberations, tell the usher."

Helga Heumann raised her head. Their eyes met as Raven passed. The usher closed the jury-room door on the eight men and four women. The table was cluttered with papers, cigarette packages, and plastic cups. A fan droned on a wall-bracket. It was twenty minutes past three. A hiccough in the plumbing system caused the lavatory cistern to flush without discernible reason.

Raven slung his alpaca jacket on the back of the chair by the window. Sweat sealed his shirt to his shoulder-blades. He lit a Gitane and watched the pungent blue smoke swirl outside.

Two police vehicles were parked in the cul-de-sac below, the drivers leaning against the sunbaked wall. Harvey Bullock dragged a chair close to Raven. The rest of the jurors stayed at the table. The blonde hairdresser returned to her game of Patience.

Sweat showed in the roots of the foreman's hair. There was a network of tiny veins in the folds of his nostrils. He lowered his voice, building a fence around them that excluded the others.

"You're not being reasonable," he said. Raven figured the foreman for some gung-ho Captain of School who had carried his conviction of personal glory into later life. "My opinion's based on what we've heard in court."

The foreman nodded impatiently: "Which is exactly what all of us have heard. You're the only one out of step. We've got a duty to return a verdict that's based on the evidence."

"You don't have to lecture me on civics or law," said Raven. "There's only one real problem, you can't get me to think as you do."

The foreman drew a long breath. "Believe me, I wouldn't be wasting my time if it wasn't a matter of principle. If the jury system is going to survive it's got to be taken seriously."

Raven leaned back in his chair. "I know a lot more about the jury system than you do. The truth is you're a natural hangman."

The foreman's neck reddened: "You're an offensive bastard, you know, and come to think of it—I'm not entirely sure that an ex-cop is supposed to sit on a jury."

"Ask the judge:" Raven invited. "I'd like to see you making a fool of yourself."

Bullock assumed the appearance of a man stripped of authority without knowing why.

"Look, we've all listened to precisely the same evidence," he repeated, "and eleven of us have reached the same conclusion."

Raven flicked his cigarette-butt through the open window and checked its safe arrival. "All I'm doing is exercising my right to hold a minority opinion. It isn't a perfect world."

The foreman shook his head: "You're a troublemaker, that's what you are: What is it with you and this girl? Do you fancy her or something?"

Raven grinned. "I'm a happily married man with a wife who wouldn't take kindly to infidelity. The truth's much simpler. I happen to know what goes on out there, the way judges and lawyers think. Above all I know how a cop's mind works. "You've all decided that this girl is guilty. I think she's innocent."

The foreman barked a laugh. It was the sort of laugh that accompanies the dirk in the back.

"Just what are you after, Raven?"

"Let's call it job-satisfaction," said Raven. "I'm trying to put this girl on the street where she belongs. But it looks as though I've lost."

"Because you are not using logic," said Bullock. "Listen, *one* of them has to be lying! Their stories are diametrically opposed."

"She doesn't *have* a story!" said Raven. "She hasn't called any evidence. All she's done is plead not guilty and sit there, not saying a word. If you had any real knowledge of what happens out there in the world you'd know that Pelham set her up. There she was, alone in a foreign country and not, I suggest, too bright. Then she meets Pelham. She was a goner from that moment on."

"It doesn't work," the foreman objected. "If she's innocent, why hasn't she gone in the box and said so?"

"Because she isn't like you and me," answered Raven. "She's one of these romantics who believes in people. She's waiting for Pelham to stand up and play the white man: In other words, she's still in love with him."

Someone slammed the lavatory door harder than was warranted. It was the blonde hairdresser, her voice a resentful whine.

"I heard what the judge said. Ten against two. Some of us can't afford to go on like this day after day."

"Why don't you tell someone's fortune?" the foreman replied. He returned his attention to Raven. "Look, we're both men of the world. I don't know how you can fall for that Little Miss Muffet act. People who deal in drugs don't *look* like people who deal in drugs. You ought to know that! No, this woman's up to her neck in it."

His breath was fierce at close quarters and Raven averted his head.

"Some drug dealer," he ventured: "An *au-pair* whose idea of a wild time is a tea-dance at the Montcalm Hotel. Why don't you use your head? There was Prince Charming poncing around on the dance-floor, looking for someone like Helga and suddenly there she was, this daft German, ready to believe every line of the bullshit he gave her."

Raven swung one leg over another, meeting the hairdresser's glare. He continued.

"I love you, he says, just like that. And she's gone! Less than two weeks later they're on their way to Amsterdam together: This isn't some slinky nightclub queen. *Look* at her for criss-sakes! This is a lonely kid ready to open her arms and legs to the first man who looks the part and makes the right noises. Dope-dealer?" He mocked the suggestion.

The foreman was unmoved. "She was alone there with his car in Amsterdam. It was perfect. She ran it into some back street garage, and out it came, a few hours later, with a million pounds worth of heroin hidden under the floorboards."

"Eight hundred thousand pounds' worth," Raven corrected. "Just to keep the record straight. Have you finished?"

The veins swelled in Bullock's neck and his eyes receded. "No, I have *not* finished! She drives from Holland to Ostend and puts Pelham's car on the ferry to Dover. And that's when she starts playing cute. Driving into the Red Channel in the Customs Shed. I ask myself *why?* The car belonged to her boyfriend, her papers were in order."

"She probably didn't even notice. She's a foreigner, remember."

The foreman's smile was superior. "She knew all right. This was Little Miss Muffet again pulling the wide-eyed act to disarm the Customs officers. But luckily it didn't work. Something clicked in that officer's head: Who knows how their minds work?"

"With suspicion," said Raven.

"Anyway they got her out of the car and stuck it on the weighbridge. It was exactly right for the year and the model. They're just about to wave her through when someone had the bright idea of taking off the wheels and weighing them. Each wheel was supposed to go 9.25 kilos. These were barely six. They were made of some sort of high-tech alloy instead of steel. The difference in weight was the dope. You heard what the man from Forensics said, Iranian heroin ninety per cent pure." There was no doubt that the foreman believed what he was saying.

"What about Pelham's behaviour?" Raven asked. "You don't find it strange? They go to Amsterdam at his suggestion and as soon as they get there he flies back to London."

Bullock pulled a face: "You heard. His mother's in a wheelchair, crippled with osteo-arthritis."

"And has been, for eight years," said Raven. "He didn't want to see his mother. He wanted to be out of firing range. Let me ask you a question. Suppose you'd lived with a woman, even for a couple of weeks. Suddenly the two of you are sitting side by side in a courtroom charged with the same offence. All she's saying is that she didn't do it. She's not putting the blame on you. Wouldn't you look at her, touch her, acknowledge her existence?"

The foreman spoke with some heat. "Would *you?* A woman who has dragged you into a mess like this! Pelham didn't *need* to get mixed up with drugs. You heard what the accountant said. Pelham was making a good living dealing in property."

"Greed:" said Raven. "We're all tinged with it, some more than others. No, I have my opinion. The girl's innocent and Pelham is guilty and that's all there is to it."

The foreman wiped the inside of his collar, his expression exasperated.

"She went to that tea-dance dressed for the part. Little Miss Muffet again! OK, Pelham was probably feeling randy but the point is that she was there with the express purpose of picking up someone like him, someone with a car and an address in this country."

"Bullshit," said Raven. "Where are the people behind this sophisticated hooker? She's been almost five months in jail waiting trial yet not a soul has been near her. And what about their defence? He's got the top man in the business while she has to go with some boy-scout from Legal Aid. You watch too much television."

"I don't even own a set," said the foreman. "As for nobody visiting her, what of it? She cooked-up the deal."

Raven brushed the ash from his trousers. "We're wasting one another's time. Let's go back in front of the judge."

"That's your final word, is it?"

"The bottom line," answered Raven.

Bullock clapped his hands together. "OK, people, let's take a vote! How many of us find Helga Heumann guilty on both counts?" Ten hands rose with his. "How many of us find Pelham not guilty on both counts?" The hands lifted again in unison.

Raven slipped into his jacket. The usher opened the door in answer to Bullock's knock. The courtroom hushed as the jurors entered. Raven returned to his seat near the dock. Neither defendant looked in his direction. The Clerk of the Court billowed to her feet.

"Have you reached a verdict, members of the jury?"

The foreman tightened his shoulder muscles. "We have, Your Honour!"

The Clerk touched the back of her neck. The gesture was graceful and feminine in spite of her bulk.

"Count One in the indictment. Do you find the defendant Piers Pelham guilty or not guilty?"

The foreman's voice was rich with importance. "Not guilty!"

"Count Two in the indictment. Do you find the defendant Piers Pelham guilty or not guilty?"

"Not guilty," Bullock repeated.

All heads turned towards the dock. Pelham flashed a thumbs-up sign at the public gallery.

"You may go, Mister Pelham." Judge Salter's voice was courteous.

Pelham was on his feet already, pumping the warder's hand. He smiled his way out of court, followed by his legal advisers. Helga Heumann and the wardress were left in the dock, the older woman standing at the German girl's shoulder.

The Clerk's tone gathered vibrancy. "Count One in the case of Helga Heumann. Do you find the defendant guilty or not guilty?"

"Guilty!" Bullock raised his chin. A man did his duty.

"Count Two in the indictment. Do you find the defendant Helga Heumann guilty or not guilty?"

"Guilty." Bullock sat down.

The judge slid his hand along his jawline. His smile exposed long yellow teeth.

"This has been a long and sometimes tedious trial, members of the jury. You have performed your duty splendidly."

The foreman made a purse of his mouth. All that was needed now, thought Raven, was a round of applause.

Judge Salter continued amiably. "The time has come for me to tell you to go to your homes. Anyone wishing to remain in court may do so, of course."

He studied the papers in front of him as the jurors collected their belongings. They passed through the exit, leaving Raven sitting alone on the front bench. The court had half-emptied. The only people left among the principals were Salter, the Drugs Squad detectives, Helga Heumann's lawyer, and a couple of solicitors. The courtroom regulars settled back to the thrill of hearing the sentence.

One of the Drugs Squad officers stepped into the witness-box and placed a buff folder on the ledge in front of him. He was wearing a palpable wig and a suit of some shiny material. He took the oath with the ease of familiarity.

"Herbert Haggard, Your Honour. Detective-Superintendent attached to the Drugs Squad, New Scotland Yard."

He stood at attention, awaiting the next instruction like a well-trained Labrador.

Judge Salter waved impatiently. "Go on!"

Haggard donned a pair of reading-spectacles, refreshing his memory from the file in front of him.

"The defendant is a German national, Your Honour. She was born in Düsseldorf, March twelfth, nineteen sixty-six. She attended schools in Düsseldorf between the ages of six and seventeen residing with her parents during that time. She is an only child. She left home at the age of nineteen and obtained employment as an *au-pair* with a family living in Waterloo, Belgium. She remained there until February of this year when she came to this country and was employed by a family called Winebert living in Hampstead, again as an *au-pair*. Her last address in the U.K. was Beech Avenue, Putney. There are no known previous convictions and no probation report, Your Honour."

Judge Salter frowned. "Yes, I noticed that. Have you any idea why this is, Superintendent?"

Haggard widened his stance. "I understand that Miss Heumann refused to see the Probation Officer, sir. She has also declined to see an official from the German Embassy."

The Judge leaned forward. "This is a sophisticated attempt to import a large amount of heroin into this country. Others must be involved. Have you any information about this, Superintendent?"

Haggard molded his lips. "Certain facts have been established, Your Honour. The heroin seized in this case is known to have come from Iran. Identical shipments have been entering the country over the past two years. Investigations are continuing, Your Honour."

He stepped down from the witness-box.

Heat made the varnish tacky and Raven eased himself on the bench. Helga Heumann was sitting ramrod straight, her face colorless. The judge turned to her lawyer.

"Yes, Mister Lassiter?"

The lawyer's robe hung from a shoulder as though plucked by some invisible hand.

"I find myself in some difficulty," he started uncertainly. "Miss Heumann insists that no plea in mitigation should be made on her behalf. Those are my instructions, Your Honour."

The judge's grimace ended in the folds of his cheeks. He glanced across at the girl in the dock.

"Do you understand what learned counsel is saying?"

The girl's voice was quiet and respectful. "I understand quite well, Your Honour. I thank Mister Lassiter for helping me. But now it is over. There is no need to say something more."

"So be it!" The judge lost no time in proceeding to sentence. "Helga Heumann, you have been found guilty of serious offences against the laws of this country. That is to say, the importation and possession of a large amount of heroin. There is no doubt in my mind that you knew exactly what you were doing. You were engaged in this filthy business for profit. Nor have I any doubt that there were others concerned with you. You have chosen to remain silent about the part they played in this enterprise. Now the bill has come in. You will go to prison for three years, twelve months of that sentence to be suspended. In addition, I am making a recommendation that when your sentence is served you be returned to your own country."

The girl swayed on her feet, her hands hiding the color that flared in her face. The wardress touched the girl's elbow and the two women disappeared through the door to the cells.

The usher's voice was strident. "The Court will rise! This Court is adjourned until tomorrow morning at ten o'clock!"

Judge Salter collected his watch and papers and was gone. His departure was a signal for an outbreak of loud conversation as though in a classroom rid of its master. Everyone except Raven seemed to have something to say and was determined to be heard.

Raven walked to Reception. He put in his claim for his jury-fee and subsistence allowance. Twenty-two days at £16.75 came to £368.50. It was a small amount set against the £100,000 Pelham's lawyer was supposed to have earned.

He descended the steps into the glare of late afternoon, his clothes uncomfortable and stinking of sweat. He turned left into the cul-de-sac. A sign warned that this was private property. The cul-de-sac was used by police vehicles transporting prisoners. Raven had been parking there since the first day of the trial. He arrived early, shielding his car from the traffic-wardens who infested the neighbourhood like dung-beetles.

His blue Metro was the only car left in the alleyway. He wound down the windows. The vinyl tweed upholstery had baked in the sun. The Metro was new, a present from his wife, a challenge to the Saabs and Citroëns of his past. He drove it reluctantly, irked by the nearness of his head to the roof, the fact that his legs were too long for the seat.

He lit a cigarette, thinking about Helga Heumann. She'd be in Holloway Prison by now, her street-clothes exchanged for the uniform of a convicted prisoner. It was years since he'd been in the women's prison but he remembered it well as a place where granite-faced wardresses rattled keys and banged doors. It was difficult to get the girl out of his mind.

He drove home by way of Fulham Road, picking up smoked ham, pickles, and watercress in the Polish delicatessen. He left his car in the alleyway by the side of his neighbour's gift shop. The shop was shut as it usually was in summer. A flyspecked card hung in the window. BACK IN HALF-AN-HOUR (OR THEREABOUTS).

Behind the windows was Lauterbach's stock-in-trade. Siamese silver and silk, devil-masks from Burma. Gongs, flutes, and incense-burners; giant jars from Aladdin's Cave.

Raven waited for the lights to change then sprinted across

the Embankment. A hot summer had left the grass brown in Battersea Park, the birds fat and glossy. The small flotilla of boats wore a festive air, decorated with bunting and pennants for the forthcoming regatta. He descended the granite steps and unlocked a door that was festooned with razorwire. A gangway gave access to the *Albatross*. The river ran sluggishly. It was low tide and a duck paddled along near a strip of mud, spooning the weeds with its bill.

Kirstie Raven was in Yugoslavia taking pictures for Italian *Vogue*. She had been gone for ten days and was due home after the weekend. The Ravens' pattern of life allowed each a large measure of freedom that strengthened the bond between them. It was Kirstie's theory that nothing kills romance quicker than too much propinquity. Raven agreed.

The *Albatross* was a converted barge that had once hauled barley from East Anglian ports to the Thameside breweries. It had been repainted that spring. The colour was Kirstie's choice, a Chinese white that Raven was still unsure about. The barge was sixty feet long with an eighteen-foot beam. The hull had been decked and a red cedarwood superstructure added. The accommodation was spacious. There were two bedrooms joined by a bathroom, a large kitchen, and a thirty-foot-by-twelve livingroom. This room was surrounded on three sides by a panoramic sweep of double glazing. Old truck tyres served as fenders, creaking and groaning as the boat strained against the pull of the mooring-chains. Roses that Kirstie had bought at Chelsea Flower Show flourished in oak tubs bolted to the deck.

Hank Lauterbach was lying on the deck of the neighbouring boat, his feet pillowed on the back of the Great Dane. An acrid smell of hash fired the light breeze. Raven coupled a length of hose to the tap and washed the deck free of gull-shit. He detested both seagulls and pigeons alike. The gulls, as hunters, become scavengers, the pigeons for their knowing guttersnipe ways, always a flutter ahead of his toe.

He unlocked the door to the livingroom. Mrs. Burrows had

left the curtains closed and it was cool inside. Coming home always gave him a feeling of satisfaction. Diffused sunlight gave a patina to the surface of his Queen-Anne desk. The much-darned Aubusson looked shabby in summer but the colours still glowed. Shelves and cupboards held an untidy collection of books, tapes, and records. The only painting hanging was his Klee, the abstract shapes a constant challenge to his imagination.

Mrs. Burrows had left the customary note propped against the reading-lamp. She always excelled herself during Kirstie's absences, doing her best to restore life to what it had been before Kirstie's arrival. Raven's shoes were polished, missing buttons were replaced on his clothes and Mrs. Burrows cooked for him. She made batches of steak-and-kidney puddings and a raisin-studded stodge she called Autumn Surprise. He dirtied plates with whatever he was supposed to have eaten and threw the rest over the side. His marriage to Kirstie was the only thing he had done wrong during a thirteen years' long association with Mrs. Burrows, and she had an immovable faith in his need of her.

Raven ran the tape on the answering-machine. The calls recorded were unimportant. He emptied his pockets onto the bed and removed his clothes in the bathroom. The nappy alpaca jacket went into the dry-cleaners bag, his shirt and under-clothes into the laundry basket. These went to the Fulham Valeting Service. Neither Kirstie nor Mrs. Burrows cared about washing clothing. He stepped onto the scales. In spite of the heat he had gained four pounds during his stint as a juror. He ran a tub full of lukewarm water and lowered himself into it. Ten minutes later he towelled himself dry and put on a pair of cut-down jeans. He poured himself a Pimm's with all the trimmings, carried the beachbed outside and put it where the evening sun would linger. He fetched Who's Who from its shelf and laid it open on deck at the head of the sunbed, his glass beside it. He lay facedown on the bed, the sun on his shoulders. Sweat ran cold from his armpits as he read:

SALTER Gordon His Honour Judge Gordon Salter QC 1976. b. 8 April 1926 m. Helena Fitt (marr. diss. 1970) Educ. Stowe Balliol College Oxford. Served war of 1939–1945 Lieut-Commander R.N. Called to bar Middle Temple Inn 1948 Deputy-Chairman Knightsbridge Crown Court. Address 89 Kensington Square W. 8. Recreations sailing horse-racing. Clubs Savile.

CULROSS Mark QC 1978 b. 7 Dec. 1927 m Ingrid Houghton 1958 Educ. Eton Magdalen College Oxford. Called to bar Middle Temple Inn 1960 SE Circuit. Recreations Theatre birdwatching. Clubs Carlton.

BERTRAM John QC b. 10 June 1923. Educ. Stonyhurst. Served Royal Corps of Signals 1941–1945. Called to bar Middle Temple Inn 1950. Treasury Counsel 1978 SE Circuit. Recreations golf, stamp-collecting. Address Nell Gwynne House SW 3. Clubs Travellers.

There was no entry for the Legal Aid lawyer. Raven put the book back on the shelf. Hank Lauterbach yelled across the intervening water.

"Come on over, I've got something good for you!"

The plank connecting the two boats was rope-lashed and Raven negotiated it gingerly. Once at the end of an evening, he had stepped from the plank into mid-air, landing in icy-cold water that shocked him sober. The Great Dane's tail thudded welcome on the dirty deck. The American was reclining on a beanbag dressed in a pair of garish Hawaiian shorts. He extended an arm, offering the joint to Raven.

Lauterbach was as tall as Raven with narrow shoulders and the thighs and legs of an anorexic dancer. He had a bushy head of brown hair and a beard that was dyed pea-green. The colour was varied from time to time. His granny glasses were on deck beside him. His eyes had an oddly naked look without them. Strains of Brubeck's "Take Five" rose from below deck.

Raven dragged on the joint, retaining the smoke in his lungs before exhaling.

"Well that's that," he said. "It's over. They found her guilty on both counts and the judge gave her three years!"

"No shit!" Lauterbach found the bitch's rump with his bare feet. "That's bad. What about the boyfriend?"

"He walked."

Lauterbach was a throwback to Flower Power days, a battler on the campuses, a veteran of Protest The System marches. Son of a Sausalito lawyer, he had accepted his father's valetudinarian broadside and the check for twenty thousand dollars that accompanied it. The note was brief. *Get out and stay out!*

London had been Lauterbach's first stop on the Great European Adventure. Ten years later he was still in the city selling his Oriental exotics. A staunch friend, generous by nature, Lauterbach had a genuine dislike of all forms of hard work.

He rolled over, his face curious. "How come they convicted her? I thought you were a holdout for an acquittal."

"I was," said Raven. "We were out for five hours and couldn't agree so the judge sent us back again. Said he'd accept a majority verdict. And that's what he got, eleven to one. We've sent an innocent woman to jail and let the real culprit go free. That, my friend, is called justice."

Lauterbach wagged his head, his beard towelling his chest. Raven's speech seemed to disturb the American's memory.

"The bastards deal and we play the cards. What the hell, John, you did your best."

"That doesn't help Helga Heumann," said Raven. "She never had a prayer from the start. Everyone except me was against her including this prick who'd elected himself foreman of the jury. He would have hanged his own mother." The first hit of the hash rolled Brubeck's piano into Raven's head and he closed his eyes. The cover on the beanbag smelled strongly of dog.

"It's an illusion," said Lauterbach.

Raven opened his eyes. "What's an illusion?"

Lauterbach waved expansively. "The whole number."

Raven sucked at the joint and passed it back. "It wasn't an attractive thing to watch, Hank. This bastard sat next to her in the dock for two weeks without a single word or a look for her.

Not one sign of recognition. He left the courtroom waving and smiling like some megastar. He didn't even stay to find out what happened to her."

"A scumbag!" Lauterbach pitched the roach over the side.

"I'll tell you something odd," said Raven. "The judge, the prosecuting counsel, and the guy who defended Pelham are all members of the same Inn of Court. I've got this feeling that they came to an arrangement."

Lauterbach made an arm for his granny glasses. "What kind of arrangement?"

"A deal. Pelham goes free and the girl is convicted."

The American gave it some thought. "How could that be?" he asked finally. "The judge wouldn't know what verdict the jury would reach."

The dope left a feeling of genial superiority in Raven's brain. "Have you ever been busted, Lauterbach?"

"You know I have," said the American.

"And been in front of a judge and jury?"

Lauterbach notched up his spectacles. "No judge and jury, no. My busts were for meatball raps. Riotous assembly, refusal to disperse when so ordered. This kind of stuff. They just throw you in a tank and let you hang out to dry."

The *Albatross* looked good from where Raven lay on the beanbag. He narrowed his eyes, enjoying the sight. When he first bought the barge there had been six other boats in the Reach. Now there were seventeen and the moorings were full.

"Well it's a whole lot different in front of a judge," said Raven. "In the first place there's this bit where he tells the jury that *they* are the judges of facts, he's only there to determine the law. And as far as it goes that's the truth. But what about the performances that go on?" I mean I've *watched* them, Hank! OK, you think of a judge sitting up there diddling himself, waiting for the moment when he either has to sentence the guy in the dock or release him. It isn't as simple as that. A judge can ask a witness a question at any time and believe me they do! Their big moments come when they make their summations. They don't like something a witness has said then we get the wagging of the head, the don't-believe-this-shit look on their faces."

Lauterbach was rolling another joint, listening. Raven sat up.

"Helga Heumann never took the stand, right? She didn't call a single witness. Let me tell you how the judge dealt with that. 'The law does not require the defendant to call evidence on her behalf, members of the jury. Still less does it require *her* to give evidence. Nevertheless, you may think it significant that no one has heard her side of the story. She stands here, pleading not guilty but refusing to defend herself. This is her legal right, of course. But is this a case where innocence is its own shield or does she fear that her case may be jeopardized by cross-examination? It's entirely a matter for you to decide.' And so on."

Lauterbach lit the joint and inhaled. "You can't win."

"Exactly," said Raven. "And this is the judge speaking, remember. It makes an impression, I've been there."

"Why didn't she give her side of the story?"

Raven shook his head, refusing the second smoke. "Because the only way she knew to defend herself was by accusing the man sitting next to her. And she just couldn't bring herself to do it. That verdict's wrong. I *know* that it's wrong!"

The Great Dane seized the EasiChew bone and lumbered below with it.

"That's a hint," Lauterbach said, getting up. "It's her supper-time. When does Kirstie get back?"

Raven stared at the sky. Torn ribbons of cloud showed to the west. "I'm not sure yet. Monday or Tuesday, I think."

The American combed through his beard with his fingers. "Don't you get lonely without her?"

"I'm always lonely without her. It makes things better when she does get back."

"What are you doing tonight? Do you want to eat here?"

"I'd like that," said Raven, rising in turn. "I'll bring the food. I picked up some stuff at the deli." It would be good to have company, something that would help get Helga Heumann out of his thoughts.

As far as he knew he had only put one innocent person inside. Even then the man had been self-convicted, a victim of the wrong choice of place and company. By the time Raven knew the truth it was too late to stop the machinery. He imagined the desolation of someone who hears sentence pronounced and knows that he's innocent. The phone began ringing as he stepped aboard the *Albatross*. It was Kirstie.

"And how is my favorite man?"

"Pissed off," he replied. "I'm out of work. The trial ended today. The girl was convicted."

His wife took the news in her stride. "Poor thing! Listen, darling, we're in Vienna. Maggie had to see someone here. We'll be back on Tuesday. OS 451 arriving at Heathrow ten twenty-five. Can you meet us?"

"Didn't you hear what I just said?" he demanded.

She kissed him over the line. "Yes, darling, I did. And I'm sorry. I know how you felt."

"She didn't do it," he said obstinately. "The kid's innocent."

"Yep!" she said briskly and changed the subject. "So what are you going to do with yourself now that you're no longer a juror?"

Her voice was a little too casual. There had been a lot of talk recently about Raven finding a hobby, something to occupy his mind. Writing a book, for instance. With all his experience and so forth.

"I don't know what I'm going to do," he said. "And if you've got something in mind I don't want to hear about it. How did your work go?"

"Just fine," she replied. "Maggie was concentrating for once so we finished ahead of schedule. We ducked the festivities in Sarajevo and came on here. I miss you, lover."

"Piffle," he said. "Stuffing yourselves with cream-gateaux and having your hands kissed. I'll be at Heathrow ten twenty-five on Tuesday."

He went into the kitchen and pulled the refrigerator to one side. A brass ring was sunk in the oak floor. He pulled on the ring, lifting a section of wood and linoleum. Steps led down to the hold. He felt for the light-switch. The timbers still smelled like a brewery. There were no windows below. The lights shone on unused paintings and furniture, things that had come from Kirstie's home in Toronto. A door led to her darkroom. On the right were his wineracks. Thermostatically-controlled heating held the hold at an even temperature. He climbed the steps with a couple of bottles of claret. He dragged the refrigerator back in place, donned a gingham shirt and a pair of brokenbacked sandals, and picked up the phone in the bedroom.

Maureen O'Callaghan answered. "It's me," said Raven. "Is he there?"

"He's in the study," she said, "but I warn you he's not in the best of moods. Trouble in court, I gather."

"That makes two of us," Raven said. "May I talk to him?"

His friend picked up. "Who else but you would choose the very moment when I'm trying to think of a way to tell a client that he's got to pay his ex-wife six hundred pounds a month! A woman he'd gladly dismember. Six hundred quid a month until she drops dead or remarries, whichever comes first."

"Think of this as an errand of mercy," said Raven. "I just left Knightsbridge Crown Court. They found Helga Heumann guilty."

"I can't say I'm entirely surprised," said the lawyer. "With someone like Salter sitting there's no need for a prosecutor. How long did he give her?"

"Three years, twelve months of it suspended."

"It could have been worse," said the lawyer. "There's a directive out to crack down on heroin offences. What about Pelham?"

"He left court without a stain on his character. It was a majority verdict. I was the holdout."

"What else?" asked the lawyer. "What do you want from

me, a professional opinion? You were lucky to get out of Salter's court without being held in contempt."

"Shall I tell you what I'd really like from you?" Raven said. "I'd like a little compassion for Helga Heumann. She didn't *do* it, Patrick! You know the case, you've read the newspapers. What sort of chance would she have on appeal?"

"None," the lawyer said promptly. "In fact the Court of Appeal might well increase her sentence: Why, is that what she has in mind?"

The effect of the joint was wearing off, leaving Raven sensitive to opposition.

"I've no idea what she has in mind," he said starchily.

"When does Kirstie get back?" asked O'Callaghan.

"You're the second person who's asked that question in the last ten minutes. People seem to be more interested in Kirstie than they are in me."

"She's prettier than you are," said the lawyer. "And come to think of it, nicer. May I go now?"

"Gladly," said Raven. "I'll talk to you when you're in a better frame of mind."

He carried the food and wine across to the neighbouring boat. Lauterbach was below. The living-quarters were cramped, just a cabin and galley. The double bunk was hung with mosquito-netting. The Great Dane was demolishing a two-pound can of MarrowMeat. The American came from the galley, watching the dog fondly.

"She always makes it *look* so good!"

Raven put the food on the table and opened one of the wine-bottles. He sniffed at the cork and looked round.

"Haven't you got any decent glasses?" Those on the table had been stolen from the pub on the Embankment.

"What's the matter with those?" Lauterbach asked. "They're the ones we always use."

Raven wrapped a cloth around the neck of the bottle and poured. "Chateau Latour in dirty pint pots. What are we eating the food on, tin plates?"

They ate for the most part in silence until Lauterbach looked at his watch.

"Time for the news." He activated the remote control for the television-set. A picture built on the screen. The announcer's voice was matter-of-fact.

"Here are the news headlines. A summit meeting has been arranged in Geneva later this year. A six-year-old girl gets a heart-transplant. Oil-tanker founders in the Bay of Biscay. Woman prisoner kills herself in Holloway Prison."

Raven swung round facing the screen. His fork fell to the floor unheeded. The announcer was in full-swing, sweating through his makeup.

". . . summit meeting will be preceded by preliminary discussions about procedure. Sara Alcott, a six-year-old girl from Grayshott in Hampshire was given a new heart today in Papworth Clinic. A spokesman for the Clinic said that Sara had responded well to the operation and although in intensive care there were high hopes for her recovery." A library shot of Holloway Prison replaced the announcer's picture. His voice continued. "Helga Heumann, a twenty-two-year-old German national bled to death in her cell in Holloway Prison late this afternoon. The woman had previously been sentenced to three years imprisonment at Knightsbridge Crown Court for offences involving heroin. A Home Office spokesman said that Heumann had severed her wrists with a metal comb. An enquiry is being held into the fatality."

Lauterbach silenced the set. Raven pushed his plate away, his appetite gone.

"I don't want any more," he said, rising.

The American's face was concerned. "Where are you going? Look, why don't you stay here?" he urged.

Raven was already halfway up the stairs. "Forget it, Hank. Look, I don't want to talk. I'll see you tomorrow!"

He sat in his kitchen with copies of the indictments spread out in front of him.

INDICTMENT No: 1987253

The Crown Court at KNIGHTSBRIDGE

THE QUEEN –v– Piers Pelham and Helga Heumann charged as follows:

Count 1 *Statement of Offence*

Possessing a controlled drug with intent, contrary to Section 5(3) of the Misuse of Drugs Act 1971, namely

Particulars of Offence

Piers Pelham and Helga Heumann had in their possession on the 18 day of April a controlled drug specified in Class A of Schedule 2 of the Misuse of Drugs Act, 1971, namely a quantity of diamorphine with intent to supply it to another.

Count 2 *Statement of Offence*

Importing a controlled drug contrary to Section 4 of the Misuse of Drugs Act 1971

Particulars of Offence

Piers Pelham and Helga Heumann on the 18 day of April imported and had in their possession a controlled drug specified in Class A of Schedule 2 of the Misuse of Drugs Act 1971 namely a quantity of diamorphine.

N. Parrott An Officer of the
Crown Court.

Raven had scribbled the word "guilty" beside Pelham's name, "not guilty" next to Helga Heumann's. He had done this during the judge's summation. He tore the indictment into small fragments and watched them sail downstream.

The angle of the dying sun cast shadow on the starboard side of the boat. Raven dragged a deck-chair to the other side. He sat with his thoughts until the phone rang. It was O'Callaghan.

"I watched the news. I'm sorry, John. A very unpleasant business. I know what you must be feeling."

"For your sake I hope that you don't," Raven answered. "Those bastards are responsible for her death, Patrick, just as surely as if *they'd* cut her wrists. Murderers, every one of them. The judge, the police, and the jury!"

"You're taking this too much to heart," said his friend. "You've got to get things in right perspective."

The light was fading fast, softening the outline of the buildings on the far side of the river. O'Callaghan was a good and sensitive man but the law inhibited his feelings.

Raven's sense of outrage exploded. "What the hell are you talking about, 'done all I could!' The girl's dead, for crissakes! She lay there in some stinking cell watching her life ooze away!"

"We don't make the rules," the lawyer said gently.

"Sod the rules!" said Raven and put the phone down.

He slept fitfully, getting up and drinking glass after glass of juice, finally moving into the guestroom. The early sun crept through the bird-patterned curtains. He struggled into a sitting position, forcing his eyes open. It was half-past seven by the clock on the wall. He threw the sheet back and went into the kitchen, resigned to the fact that his first thoughts were of Helga Heumann. He ground coffee-beans in the mill, filled the percolator, and went out on deck. It was quiet on the river, the air clean and unused. The only sign of life came from the boats with children. It was too early for the roar of overhead traffic. The length of hose was still attached to the tap. Raven watered the roses, the deck steaming gently.

He collected the newspapers from the box outside the gangway. He spread them out on the table, coffee by his side. *The Times* devoted three lines to Helga's suicide. The style of the tabloid was more florid.

DRUGS DEALER TAKES OWN LIFE

Helga Heumann, a German national from Düsseldorf, did herself to death in a lonely cell in Holloway Prison yesterday. Heumann, 22, a blonde *au-pair*, had been sentenced earlier to three years in Knightsbridge Crown Court for importing heroin with a street value of £800,000. The owner of the Mercedes used in the crime, Old Etonian Piers Pelham, was acquitted of similar charges. Interviewed at his swank £250,000 home in Putney's Beech Avenue, Pelham refused to comment on his relationship with the dead German woman. Detectives from the Central Drugs Squad are thought to be looking for an Iranian dope-ring said to be based on the Continent. Police sources reveal that they have been deeply concerned by the increasing amount of heroin coming into the country.

There was a picture of Pelham taken on the steps outside Knightsbridge Crown Court, a triumphant smile on his face.

Raven put his coffee-bowl in the sink and went back to bed. He knew what he had to do without being sure he could do it. He felt deeply concerned and somehow responsible. He had no idea where the dead girl's family lived or how to get hold of them. But he did know how to get hold of Pelham. What he had to do was start with the premise that Pelham was guilty. It was a while before Raven thought of a plausible excuse for going to see him.

It was after eleven o'clock by the time Raven had shaved and dressed in clean jeans and a blue, cotton shirt. Another half-hour and Mrs. Burrows would be on board with questions he was in no mood to answer. She knew that he had been serving as a juror and displayed a lively interest in the saltier details of the case. He scribbled a note for her and locked the door behind him. He walked to the end of the gangway, the empty overnight case under his arm.

Lauterbach waved from his boat. "You going to be around today?"

"It depends," Raven said vaguely. He could see the Metro still parked in the alleyway. His daily hope was that someone would steal and then wreck it.

He crossed the road and locked the empty bag and the bundle of jurors exhibits in the trunk of the Metro. He opened the windows and sun-roof. He found the Wineberts' address in the

A–Z. It was on the long hill leading up to Hampstead Heath. Refugees had flocked into the neighbourhood from Central Europe bringing their own culture with them. There were coffeehouses where the dispossessed played chess, drank Mocha, and read newspapers from home. The fringe arts flourished and there were zithers and ladies in dirndls.

Raven pulled the Metro to the kerb. The Winebert home was in the heartland of the Jewish professional classes. Raven unclipped his seatbelt. There were no parking restrictions. A Volkswagen utility was parked on the concrete front yard outside the front door.

Raven rang the bell. An attractive woman in her early thirties appeared. She was tall with a crisp cotton dress and large feet stuffed into espadrilles.

"Good morning!" smiled Raven. "Are you Mrs. Winebert?"

She nodded. "If it's my husband you're looking for I'm afraid he's left for the office."

A child's bicycle stood in the Regency-striped hallway. The same patterned wallpaper climbed with the stairs to the second storey. There was a glimpse of a baby grand piano through a door on the left of the hallway. The Victorian ugliness of the house was left outside.

"My name's John Raven," he volunteered. Years of practice had given him a sense of the right approach. "I won't beat about the bush, Mrs. Winebert. I'd like to talk to you about Helga Heumann."

"Helga?" She eyed him curiously. "If you're from the police, by chance, we've already made statements. To the Drug Squad officers."

"I'm not from the police," said Raven. "I was one of the jurors at Helga's trial. I voted for her acquittal. I thought she was innocent. I still do."

She widened the gap in the door. "Please come in!"

The room with the piano had French windows opening onto a small garden with a child's swing, hollyhocks, and a patch of grass. An architect's model of a highrise building stood on the

Steinway. Japanese prints brightened the walls. Mrs. Winebert perched on the piano-stool, displaying a good pair of legs without coquetry.

"Do please sit down!" she invited.

He took one of the velvet-backed chairs. "Do you mind if I smoke?"

She gave him an ashtray and lit a cigarette of her own.

"I want you to know how I feel," he said. "I was close enough to touch Helga, the way we were sitting in court. Five days a week for over two weeks. I was none the wiser at the end of it. I've no idea what went on in her head."

"It doesn't really matter now, does it, poor girl?" Mrs. Winebert's brown eyes were flecked with green.

"I think it does," he argued. "I'm going to do my best to find out the truth behind that trial. And the more I know about Helga, the better my chance of doing it. I'm going to clear her name, Mrs. Winebert."

She smoked as people do who are not really addicted, tapping her cigarette before the ash formed.

"And how do you propose to do that?"

"By writing a book. I know what you're thinking, but if I get it right we may get a public enquiry going. I reject most of the evidence that was given in court. I believe that Pelham was the villain of the piece. I believe that he conned Helga into making that trip."

Mrs. Winebert frowned at the floor before looking up again. "Even if you're right, I don't see how you intend to prove it. I mean, Helga's dead and that man is free. The court acquitted him."

"It can be done," Raven said with assurance. "Let me ask you something, Mrs. Winebert. You knew Helga well. Do *you* think she was part of some international dope-ring?"

She shook her head, smiling wryly. "Helga was a total romantic. She didn't smoke and rarely drank. I don't quite know how to explain what I mean except that in some ways she was extremely naïve. More like fifteen than twenty-two. Incidentally I told her solicitor that I was willing to testify on Helga's behalf but she didn't want me."

He nodded. "That's part of what I mean, understanding the way she thought. My problem is that once the case is over everyone concerned closes ranks. Nobody wants to unwrap the package. You're my only point of reference."

"I don't see how I can help," she objected.

"You can help just by talking to me about Helga." He needed this woman on his side.

She was still unconvinced. "But what can I say! That we were all very fond of her?"

"You could tell me how you found her in the first place."

"That's easy," she said and opened a drawer in the bureau. The card she gave him was from a Kensington agency. "We'd had such bad luck with *au-pairs,*" she explained. "We wanted somebody special for Angelika. That's our daughter. Anyway Helga came here for an interview and I liked her at first sight. She was quiet and reserved and obviously fond of children. My daughter fell in love with her straight away."

Raven glanced out at the garden. It would be a good place for a girl like Helga to sit.

"What did Helga do with her spare time?" he asked.

Mrs. Winebert shrugged. "The problem was that she had no friends. Once in a while she'd go to the Goethe Institute if a German film was showing. Otherwise she spent most of her spare time in her room. Or watch television with us."

"What about phone-calls?"

"She had none. None that I knew about, anyway. I suppose that man must have called her towards the end of her stay here but if so she kept it secret. I find myself partly to blame when I think about him. Helga came to see me one day in a state of excitement. Someone at the Goethe had told her about these tea-dances at the Montcalm Hotel. She wanted to know what I thought."

Mrs. Winebert came to her feet smiling. "I told her that I'd never been to a tea-dance in the whole of my life and that's the truth! But it was a respectable hotel and she was after all twenty-two! I'm afraid I encouraged her."

"And what happened then?"

Mrs. Winebert sat down again. "She came back that night, full of having met this man, how charming he was, what a good dancer and so on. I didn't give it too much thought to be honest. Then a couple of days later she told us that she was getting married. I mean, that *did* worry me, especially since she refused point-blank to discuss it. She wasn't rude. Just very firm. It was her life, she said, and she knew what she was doing. That was the last time I saw her. We were out when she came to collect her things."

"She didn't leave an address?"

She moved her head from side to side. "Nothing! We didn't even know where her father was living. We knew it was Düsseldorf but not the address. My husband wanted to write to her father."

"And she left while you and your husband were out?"

"There was this thing at Angelika's dancing-school. My husband's potty about her, so we both went. Helga knew we were going. That's when she came back. Our neighbour saw her drive up in this car with Pelham. He stayed outside. We found her key on the kitchen table when we returned. That was the last we heard until the police came. Then the reporters. I tell you, that was a nightmare! Her voice faltered.

"It must have come as a shock to you?" Raven suggested. "I mean it was entirely out of character, wasn't it?"

She screwed up her face. "This is hindsight, of course, but Helga *could* be secretive. There was this business about her diary for instance. I certainly did not know it but she kept a diary. She had it with her in my daughter's room one evening. They were both watching television and I came in. The diary was lying on the bed, open. I couldn't help but see, Mister Raven! In any case the diary was written in German and I couldn't understand. Helga literally snatched it away. I mean, I thought the best thing was to ignore the whole thing. She stayed very quiet for the rest of the evening."

"Can you remember when that was?" Raven pressed.

Mrs. Winebert lit another cigarette. "It was two days before she left. The day after she'd been to the tea-dance. She made a joke of it in the morning, talking about her wicked past. She told me she'd been keeping a diary since she was eleven."

"Did she take the diary with her?"

Mrs. Winebert waved her cigarette. "I imagine so. I only saw it on the one occasion."

"Did you tell the police about it?" Excitement tugged at his voice.

She looked puzzled. "You mean about the diary? Good God, no! Do you think I should have?"

"It's probably unimportant." He smiled. "I was a policeman myself. That was a long time ago."

"Really?" The news was clearly without any impact. She glanced at her watch. "You'll have to excuse me now, Mister Raven. I have things to do."

He gave her his card. "In case you happen to think of something that might be of interest. If I'm not at home there's an answering-machine."

She opened the front door for him. Her handshake was friendly. "I'm just sorry I couldn't do more, Mister Raven. Good luck with your endeavours, anyway. The truth is we really did like Helga. My daughter still talks about her. She was heartbroken when Helga left."

The door closed. Raven moved the Metro a couple of hundred yards, unwilling that the woman might think he was spying on her. He unlocked the trunk and took out the bundle of juror exhibits. He folded his lanky body back in the driver's seat and picked the charge-sheet from the bundle. The photocopied document described the property that had been found with Helga Heumann at the time of her arrest.

1 German passport.

1 brown leather handbag containing sixteen pounds sterling, a Leicester Building Society passbook and various papers.

1 plastic compact containing lipstick and make-up.
3 car-keys.
1 yellow metal watch with plastic strap.
1 travelling-bag with a quantity of female clothing.

Helga Heumann's signature was appended to the bottom of the charge-sheet. There was no mention of a diary.

He looked at his watch. It was just before noon. He was in no particular hurry and chose a roundabout way to reach Putney. He switched on the radio, listening to France-Inter. The music reminded him of Kirstie and Paris. They used the Quai d'Anjou apartment three or four times a year. It had belonged to her dead brother and Kirstie refused to sell it. She was fiercely protective about certain areas in her life. Raven suddenly wished that she were in London instead of Vienna.

He turned the Metro east on Putney Common. Pelham's house was between Lower Richmond Road and the river. Beech trees shaded an avenue of neo-Georgian houses protected by high brick walls. Pelham's was the last on the right. Raven drove past to the bottom of the avenue and parked. A gate in the railings gave access to the grassy bank and the towpath. There was an air of rural peace about the scene. Dogs dozed in the warm dirt. Mulberries stained the pavements.

Raven unfastened the gate at the end of Pelham's driveway and started to walk towards the red brick house. The driveway finished in a graveled turning-circle. The garage doors were open, displaying the Mercedes 350 SL that had figured in the trial. Raven leaned on the bell-push. Curtains billowed in the open windows. A girl in her early twenties opened the front door. A tennis bandeau imprisoned hair with the colour and sheen of a crow's plumage. The white bikini heightened her sun-tan. She was wearing a small gold lion suspended between her breasts on a slender chain. Finger and toe nails were painted the same shade of crimson.

She stood squarely in the doorway, eyeing Raven's jeans and shirt.

"Yes?" she asked flatly.

"Mister Pelham?" he enquired. He saw into the hallway behind her. An open door led to the garden. He could see a sunbed, the end of a swimming-pool.

The girl's nose narrowed as if detecting an unpleasant odour. "Who are you, exactly?"

He kept his voice amiable. "It's a personal matter. If I could just have a word with Mister Pelham?"

She stared down the driveway. "Are you a reporter?"

"My name is John Raven," he said patiently. "I'm not a reporter."

The dialogue was interrupted by Pelham's appearance through the door at the end of the hallway. He was wearing orange swim-trunks and carrying a glass in his hand.

"What is it, Harriet?" he called.

The girl gestured, still blocking Raven's way into the house. "He says he wants to see you!"

"I'll take care of it, Pelham said easily. He loped past her, glass in hand, waiting until she had gone through the door to the garden. Recognition grew as he looked at Raven.

"I know you!" he challenged.

A stairway backlit by sunshine climbed to the second storey. There were rugs on the hallway floor.

"Can I come in?" Raven asked.

"We can talk here," said Pelham. His expression changed suddenly. "I've got it! You were one of the jurors!"

"That's right," said Raven. "Congratulations!" There was no reason why Pelham should know who the holdout had been.

Pelham emptied his glass deliberately. "You didn't come here to pass pleasantries. What do you want?"

"You're sure that we can't talk inside?" Raven asked.

"I'm sure," said Pelham. There was no flab on his sun-tanned body.

It was the smile that got to Raven. It was the smile of a man who is completely sure of himself. Only the eyes betrayed Pelham's wariness.

"I'm busy," said Pelham. "Just state your business."

Raven leaned against the door and fished for a smoke. "That was my first time doing jury-service." His lighter flared. He dropped it back in his pocket and smiled. "It was quite an experience. In fact I'm thinking of writing a book about it. That's why I'm here in fact. You could be of help to me."

"Me!" His laugh was as practised as his smile. "You're joking, of course!"

"I'm serious," Raven answered.

Pelham walked back and closed the door to the garden.

"What did you say your name was?"

"John Raven." He produced another card.

Pelham studied it. "I've just been through four months of absolute hell," he said dangerously. "And you want me to help you tell the world about it?"

Raven came off the door. "I understand how you feel but everything would be in strict confidence."

Pelham tilted his head. "What's so special about the trial?"

"It's the human angle that I find intriguing," Raven said. "It seems to me that we only heard half the story. I'm talking about Helga Heumann's story of course."

Pelham took another look at Raven's card. "What you're trying to do is capitalise on other people's misery. That's the real truth of the matter isn't it?"

"Wrong," answered Raven. "I'm trying to understand what made a girl with Helga Heumann's background go off the tracks."

"She's dead," said Pelham bluntly. "And that's all there is to it."

An ice-cream cart tinkled nearby. "I know that she's dead," Raven argued. "But the problem didn't die with her. We're living in a country with an eightfold increase in heroin addiction over the last six years. It isn't that people don't know about the problem. They're just not concerned. A story like Helga's might jolt their conscience."

"I doubt it." Pelham scratched at a sun-tanned shoulder.

"Junkies do drugs because they want to do drugs. It's as simple as that."

"I'd call that a cynical statement." Raven ground his cigarette into the gravel.

"Realistic." Pelham corrected.

There was no change in Raven's tone. "I've just been to see the people Helga worked for in Hampstead. The woman says that Helga kept a diary. I might learn some of the answers if I could get hold of it."

Pelham leaned back hard against the edge of the door, balancing the pose with the top part of his body.

"Helga didn't keep a diary." The voice was relaxed but not Pelham's eyes.

"Mrs. Winebert's sure that she did," said Raven. "It was written in German. You may not have seen it but that's understandable. A diary's a very personal thing."

Pelham glanced back at the phone on the hallway table. "I think you'd better leave!"

"Look, this wouldn't take long," Raven argued. "A couple of hours with a tape-recorder. For instance, I'd be interested to know how she impressed you when you met at that tea-dance."

Pelham's face snapped shut. "How she impressed me? She was a cheap little crook who came close to ruining my whole life. Write your sodding book but I'll tell you this much. Print one word about me and I'll sue! And believe me, I'm well placed for suing!"

He put his body behind the door and slammed it shut. Raven walked back down the driveway. Once beyond the gate, the brick wall hid him from view of the house. He fetched the empty overnight bag from the car and placed it at the foot of the wall, close to Pelham's gate. He slithered down the grassy bank to the tow-path. There was a payphone a hundred yards away. He used his handkerchief when he opened the door and dialled with the tip of a key. A woman's voice spoke.

"Which service, please?"

"Police," said Raven.

A second woman came on the line. "My name's Russell Bebb," said Raven. "I've been fishing off the tow-path at the bottom of Beech Avenue, Putney. About half-an-hour ago I saw a man put a bag down by somebody's wall on Beech Avenue. It's near the bottom. The bag's still there. You people have been asking us to report things like that."

Raven drove the Metro to the junction with Lower Richmond Road and parked in front of a church. Five minutes passed then a white police Rover appeared, traveling fast, its siren strident. Raven slid low on his shoulder-blades, still able to see the length of Beech Avenue. The Rover stopped outside Pelham's house: Two uniformed officers emerged, one speaking into his walkie-talkie. They approached the bag cautiously, peered inside. They conferred briefly and resumed their places in the car, taking the empty bag with them. The police-car drove off.

CHAPTER 2

Pelham hurried up the stairs in bare feet and stationed himself at the window. Raven was nearing the end of the driveway. Pelham watched as the tall gangling man bent down, making sure that the gate was properly fastened. Then the brick wall hid him from Pelham's view. A short while later a car drove past with Raven at the wheel.

Pelham sat down in a chair. The bedroom was a shambles. Harriet's clothes trailed from door handles, lay on the floor where she had stepped out of them. It was no better in the bathroom. She left the toothpaste uncapped, shaved her bloody legs in the tub, put lipstick all over the towels. Her kittenish charm had become a source of extreme irritation. They'd met at a party given for his release from custody. People had drifted in and out. Some clown had played boogaloo banjo. The man giving the party had been at Eton with Pelham and was passing out lines of coke as though Pelham's release on bail was the social event of the year.

The brunette in the jeans and angora sweater had been posed against the wall, her eyes following Pelham wherever he went. Lucky with women, he sensed that she would be no exception. He introduced himself and learned that she was Harriet Horne, out-of-a-job and living on an allowance from her novelist father. She talked with her eyes half-closed, still leaning against the wall. Her eyes opened suddenly.

"This is a boring party. Why don't we go somewhere else?"

Back at the house in Putney they drank more champagne while Harriet enlarged on her past. A succession of boarding-schools, her stay at the last involving an appeal to her father to remove her. The nuns found her a disruptive influence. She'd left her father's home at the age of eighteen. By this time she was on the social merry-go-round and getting her pictures in the glossies. She shared flats with friends, she said, and worried about today tomorrow. Three days later she moved in with Pelham. He found her an amusing companion and an exciting lover. That was three months ago and times had changed. She was assuming an intimacy that he'd never granted and his friends were puzzled by the relationship. The truth was he was sick of her.

He walked across the corridor to a spare room overlooking the garden. Harriet was lying naked on the sunbed, her bikini on the ground beside her. Her face was covered with a straw hat decorated with one of Pelham's ties.

The house was rented like the Mercedes in the garage. Each mail delivery brought fresh demands for Pelham to settle unpaid bills. His bank account showed a credit of seven hundred pounds.

Worry dragged his mind back to Raven. The reason for the visit was plausible enough. It was this stuff about a diary that was making him nervous. The fact that he'd never seen Helga with a diary proved nothing, as Raven had pointed out. He tried to retrace his time with her. Helga had stayed in the hotel while he went to meet Dirk Biever. The deal was set up like all the others. A mechanic arrived at the hotel and collected whatever car Pelham was driving, ostensibly for service. It was returned a few hours later with a bill that was paid by the desk. Helga couldn't have known anything about the heroin stashed under the floorboards. Pelham searched back further, remembering her stay in Putney. He'd been careful on the phone and had no visitors. They'd spent most of the time talking about his farmhouse he was supposed to be buying in Tuscany, the bloody idyllic life they would live there together. In spite of all this, the thought persisted that he might have let something slip.

The sound of a police siren had him scrambling back to the

front of the house. He reached the window in time to see the
white roof of a police-car showing over the brick wall. A couple of uniformed cops climbed out. One of them had a walkie-
talkie. Pelham stepped back smartly. Then the police-car drove
off at speed.

Pelham lowered himself on the bed, a dew of sweat breaking
out on his body. His lawyer was the first thing he thought of.
Nobody ever got into trouble keeping his mouth shut. He
wiped his neck with the edge of the sheet. His brain seemed to
have suspended its function. It took some time to pull himself
together. He knew now what he had to do.

Harriet was still lying in the same position. He removed the
hat from her face.

"I have to go out," he said. She pushed up on an elbow,
shielding her eyes from the sun with her free hand.

"Who *was* that man who came here?"

"He's called John Raven," he said. She couldn't have heard
the police-siren. "He wants to write a book about the trial."

"A *book?* I'd have thought that it's all been said."

"That's his affair." He looked down at her, smiling, at the
same time apprehensive and fearful. A man about to go on the
run probably felt like this. "I'm not sure when I'll get back.
There's some business I have to take care of."

She reached for her hat and resumed her prostrate position.
"If you're not back by six-thirty, I'll go on by myself. We're
having supper with Stephen and Michele, remember?"

"You do that," he said. "I'll probably be late." He showered
and dressed in a red-and-white striped shirt and grey silk suit.
He put his passport in his pocket, threw some clean underwear
in an overnight bag, and picked up the phone.

A hoarse voice answered "Mount's First Editions."

"I have to see you," said Pelham. His ear detected the sound
of the extension phone downstairs being lifted. He tiptoed to
the window. The sunbed was empty. Harriet came from the
hallway as he watched, still naked, carrying a magazine.

Pelham spoke into the mouthpiece again. "One o'clock, the usual place! And be there, this is important!"

He redialled and talked to a radio-cab dispatcher. "Twenty-eight Beech Avenue, Putney," said Pelham. "I'll be waiting at the gate."

He carried the bag downstairs and left it outside the front door. He walked through to the garden. Harriet lowered her magazine very slowly.

"Have fun!" she said casually. The magazine hid her face again.

"You too," he replied. With any sort of luck it would be the last time he clapped eyes on her.

He carried his bag down the driveway, keeping close to the trees and out-of-view of the pool. The cab arrived as Pelham opened the gate.

"Saint Stephen's Hospital, Fulham Road!" Pelham closed his eyes and the cab moved forward.

He'd been a chancer all his life, ready to run when the vibes were bad. He'd come close to a long stretch in the slammer but that was almost forgotten. It was the new threat that worried him. He paid off the cab in front of the hospital and carried his bag inside. He took a seat on a bench to his left. There was a brisk traffic of doctors, nurses, and patients in the entrance hall. It was five past one when a sadfaced man came through the doors from the street. He sat down beside Pelham, pulling up his trousers and displaying elastic-sided boots. His hair was wispy and grey.

He spoke like a ventriloquist's dummy. "I wish you'd make proper arrangements. This is highly inconvenient."

"Maybe so," said Pelham. "I had a visitor this morning. One of the jurors at my trial, a man called John Raven. He's writing a book about the case and he wants me to help him."

The bookdealer's expression was startled. "What sort of thing is he going to write?"

"Well," said Pelham, "he's got this idea that he should learn more about Helga Heumann, that there's a story behind her conviction."

Mount looked relieved. "That should be easy to handle. I mean, she's dead."

Pelham looked at his fingernails. "He'd just come from that place where she worked in Hampstead. The woman told him that Helga kept a diary."

An expression of alarm was fixed on the bookdealer's face. "I read the transcript of the trial. There was no mention of a diary."

Pelham continued. "Fifteen minutes after this bastard left, a squad-car arrived outside my house. Two cops. They just stood there, looking up the driveway for a few minutes then left. What do you make of that?"

Mount digested the information slowly. "There's probably some perfectly simple answer," he said finally.

"Then you look for it!" Pelham replied. "I've had enough."

Mount rocked to and fro on the bench. "You disappoint me, Piers, you really do. This attitude isn't professional."

"You have a wonderful way with words," Pelham said sarcastically.

"Well, what do you expect *me* to do?" Mount demanded. "This sort of thing isn't my concern.

The hospital smell was offending Pelham's sensibilities. "I'll tell you what I want you to do," he said. "In the first place I need to get out of this country for a bit. I don't like what's happening. And I'm broke, George. I have to have money."

Mount's tongue licked over dry lips. "What sort of money did you have in mind?"

Pelham doubled the amount he had thought of. "Twenty thousand pounds. They owe me that much. Remember, I kept my mouth shut."

Mount cleared his throat noisily. "That's a lot of money. They may well refuse. They're heavily out of pocket already."

Pelham's grin was engaging. "Then I'll have to look hard for this diary, won't I? It may be of value."

Mount's voice was back to its usual croak. "That's not the sort of joke they'll appreciate, Piers."

"Then don't tell them," Pelham said carelessly. The idea of a diary existing disturbed him deeply.

Mount dragged his eyes away from a man in robe and pajamas who was hobbling towards the elevators.

"I certainly don't have that sort of money."

"They do," said Pelham. "Tell them I want it by seven o'clock tonight. Tell them I'm very nervous."

The bookdealer's discomfort continued. "I'll pass on the message but I can't promise anything."

Pelham touched the older man's sleeve familiarly. "I don't need promises, George. I need the money. I want it in used fifties, understood? I'll be in the Gambrinus Bar at seven o'clock. It's easy to find, at the top of Sloane Avenue."

Mount placed both hands on his knees and heaved himself up. "All this sounds dangerously like blackmail to me."

Pelham mocked his expression. "I've nothing to lose, George."

Mount walked through the exit. He was moving more slowly these days, a side-effect of the pills he was taking. He stopped a cab and drove back to his bookstore. He dialled a number, hanging up as soon as he heard the ringing tone. He repeated the manoeuvre. The third time he left the line open.

"Trouble," he said. "I've just left our friend. He's asking for twenty thousand pounds."

"Does he give any reason?" The foreigner spoke English well. Mount chose his words carefully. In a sense he was cutting his own throat. Pelham was partly his production.

"The girl left a diary."

"Who says so?"

"He does. One of the jurors went to see him this morning about writing a book on the trial. The man's name is John Raven. The woman where Helga worked told Raven about the diary."

A pause preceded the question. "Do you think Pelham's lying?"

"I'm not sure," answered Mount. "But he's certainly edgy. He's complaining about some police-car that stopped outside his house."

"In other words, it's a try-on, a shakedown?"

That's what it looks like. He says he wants the money in used fifties. There's a bar near Sloane Avenue called the Gambrinus. He's going to be there at seven o'clock tonight. If you ask me, he's preparing to skip the country."

"What about this woman he's living with?"

"He didn't mention her. I know he's got debts."

"Give me the name of that juror again."

Mount did so. "If he calls again, what do you want me to say?"

"Tell him he'll get the money. And don't call this number. I'll contact you."

Mount placed the CLOSED sign in the window and went down the stairs to the basement. It was dark and cool, the glass-fronted bookcases filled with first editions in plastic wrappers. He opened the cupboard where he kept tea-bags, sugar, and milk, an electric kettle. He filled the kettle with water. His flat was up on the second floor. He had lived like this for almost five years since the rasp in his throat had been diagnosed as cancer. The consultant at the Royal Marsden had been frank. The growth was deep-seated and the treatment could only be palliative. The consultant spoke vaguely about science catching up with the disease.

Two years later Mount read an article in *The Lancet*. A professor in Bavaria was achieving remarkable results in the treatment of cancer with laser beams. Mount made enquiries. The clinic was located deep in pine woods on the south bank of the Stahrembergsee. Diagnosis was impossible without observation and tests. The fees were three hundred pounds a day, treatment and medicine included. His bill at the clinic would come to eighteen thousand pounds. At that moment his stock and the money he had in the bank amounted to no more than two-thirds of the amount.

He flew to Munich where a car from the clinic awaited him. He spent a week undergoing tests. The results claimed that his condition would respond to treatment but would require a stay of at least four months. Mount came back to England. A collector of Graham Greene firsts brought an Iranian friend to the store. The talk ranged from books to death and then cancer. A couple of weeks later another Iranian appeared. He had a solution to Mount's financial problems. All he had to do was to act as a sort of post-box, pass on messages. There was no risk and he would be well paid for each operation. It took a day for Mount to make up his mind. He now had more than half the money he needed in a special account. A few more deals would add another generation to his lifetime. Meanwhile he lived frugally in three rooms over the store.

Pelham stopped at a Chinese restaurant on King's Road. The interior was decorated with bamboo, gilt, and red-lacquered dragons. He used his chopsticks expertly, washing down crabmeat, ginger, and fried rice with a pint of Holsten. The last hour had given him a new sense of freedom. He found himself almost grateful for Raven's visit. Shock had nudged him into taking a decision he should have taken weeks ago. Pack a bag and walk away from it all.

The more he thought about Helga's diary, the stronger became his belief in its existence. It was the sort of thing that a fool like Helga would have done. The police-car no longer worried him. As Mount said, it was probably a coincidence. He spent the next two hours in a movie-theatre and emerged into late-afternoon sunshine. He called his home number. There was no reply. Ah well, Harriet had a shock coming! As soon as he got his money, he'd take a cab to the airport and buy a ticket on the first flight that took his fancy.

Five to seven. He walked into the Gambrinus. The walls were hung with abstract paintings. The customers were young and decorative. Two large rooms were joined by half-a-dozen steps. Pelham chose a table that commanded a view of the entrance. He ordered a glass of wine and settled back. He was suddenly aware of a man watching him from the top of the stairs. He was slim, dark, and dressed in a light-grey suit. His eyes were hidden behind sun-glasses. He descended the steps and extended his hand.

"Please come with me," he said in accented English. "The car is outside."

Pelham took his bag from the floor. The street was hot after the air-conditioned bar. The stranger pointed at an Alfa-Romeo parked on the other side of the street. The rear door opened as the two men approached. The man sitting on the back seat was a few years older than his companion and darker in hue. He was wearing a pink shirt, no jacket, and his slacks were held up with a Gucci belt.

"Rest assured," he said, showing good teeth. "You are with friends. I am Saladin."

The driver swung left and headed down Sydney Street. Pelham had a quick tinge of uneasiness.

"Where are we going?"

Saladin placed a hand on Pelham's sleeve. "Be patient, Mister Pelham. Twenty thousand pounds is a lot of money to carry around."

They were crossing Battersea Bridge. Family groups with children and dogs were walking towards the park. The driver's eyes found the rearview mirror. The two men spoke in a language that had the guttural sound of Arabic. Saladin smiled reassuringly at Pelham. They passed Wandsworth Common with its dusty bushes, fouled hollows, and bleak railroad tracks. Women with saris gossiped in doorways. They were in law-abiding Asian territory now. The car stopped outside a pebble-and-dash house. Plaster gnomes cemented into the ground. A FOR SALE sign rose from the brickwork. The driver took a dispatch-case from the seat beside him and opened the door.

"This won't take long," Saladin said easily. The skin over his cheekbones was pocked with old smallpox scars. He took Pelham's bag and opened the door to the house with a key on a ring bearing an estate-dealer's label. They stepped into a bare hallway covered with dingy linoleum. The house had the airless smell associated with unopened windows. Saladin shut the kitchen door behind them. The only furniture was a kitchen table and two chairs. Saladin emptied the contents of Pelham's bag onto the table. His companion lowered a venetian blind on the window and snapped on a naked bulb in the ceiling. Saladin was inspecting each article of Pelham's clothing.

Pelham managed to find his voice. "What the hell's going on here?"

Saladin swung round, levelling a .38 automatic at Pelham's middle.

"Take off your clothes, shoes, and socks!"

He checked the contents of Pelham's pockets, retaining the passport and credit cards. He rapped each shoe smartly on the floor.

"Sit on the chair!"

The other man plugged in an electric kettle and placed a tin bowl on the drainingboard. He opened his dispatch-case and donned a white surgical smock.

"The gentleman is a qualified doctor," said Saladin.

The doctor started to draw out objects from his case with the deftness of a conjuror. Pelham noted each item produced with growing terror. A scalpel and what looked like a nutcracker went into the pan of boiling water. A stethoscope appeared, adhesive tape and gauze dressings, a bottle of pure alcohol.

Pelham made an attempt to leave the chair. He collapsed as Saladin raised the gun again. The doctor put the stethoscope against Pelham's chest, checked his pulse-rate, and fastened an inflatable rubber band round Pelham's left arm. He pumped the band taut and spoke in Farsi to Saladin.

Saladin translated. "He says you're in very good shape. The constitution of a tiger. We are going to remove the tip of a finger. Every precaution will be taken. Which hand do you prefer?"

The question left Pelham speechless. He had been strapped to the chair with adhesive tape, his left arm dangling free.

Saladin smiled benignly. "The less you struggle, the sooner it's over."

The doctor swabbed the inside of Pelham's left forearm with alcohol and plunged the contents of a hypodermic syringe into a vein. The effect was immediate. His arm became dead from the elbow down. He saw his hand laid on the wooden table. Pelham averted his head, biting his lip, tears in his eyes. The crunch told him that the joint had been severed. He sagged in his chair, held by the tightly wrapped tape. When he opened his eyes again his hand had been dressed. The top joint was missing from his little finger. The doctor fitted a glove-stall. Pelham felt no pain yet, just shock and outrage. Saladin slashed through the tape with a scalpel and held a flask to Pelham's lips. Brandy ran down Pelham's chin.

"You can put your clothes on again," said Saladin.

Pelham struggled into his shirt and trousers. The two men were speaking in Farsi again, the doctor mopping blood from the table top. There was an air of informality about them, as though Pelham had just had a tooth extracted. The doctor dropped the severed fingertip in a plastic bag, emptied the bloodied water down the sink, and repacked his dispatch-case. The street door closed behind him.

Saladin pocketed his .38. He lit two cigarettes and passed one to Pelham. Pelham used his right hand, fingers shaking. The first wave of pain exploded in his nervous system.

"You're not just a liar," said Saladin. "You're a fool! This is a very serious business. And what you have to understand is that once you're in, it's forever. You belong to us now. You can hide from the police, your friends, and your enemies, but we'll always find you."

"You're making a big mistake," Pelham said unsteadily.

"Those bastards from the Drugs Squad kept me in a cell for three days, trying to get me to talk. I kept my mouth shut."

The blind rattled up, filling the room with light. "If you want to keep your other fingers intact," Saladin said, "you'll have to continue to give us your loyalty."

Pelham wiped his mouth with the back of his good hand. "I keep telling you, you've always had it."

"I want the truth about the girl's diary," Saladin said.

Pelham could hear the sound of children outside on the street. "I don't know what I'm supposed to say," he objected. "I've never seen any diary."

Saladin's pock-marked face seemed to grow in size. "Do you think that Raven has got it?"

Pelham was close to tears. The pain had extended beyond his hand, invading his entire body.

"I don't know," he said.

Saladin narrowed his gaze. "This woman in Hampstead has no motive to lie. You lived with Helga Heumann for two weeks. You must have seen her diary."

"I don't believe this," Pelham said despairingly. "Look, if there *is* a diary, it's of no consequence. Helga saw nothing. She didn't even *know* what was going on."

Saladin persisted. "You came here tonight asking for money. Was that because you thought you had some sort of insurance?"

Pelham licked his dry lips. "I came here because I'm scared. And that's the truth."

"Twenty thousand pounds?" The Iranian's smile was ironic. "Do you take me for a fool? Either you have the diary or you know where it is."

"You're wrong," said Pelham, "Maybe Raven's got it. I don't *know!*" he repeated.

Saladin changed tack. "How much have you told this other woman, the one you're living with now?"

"Harriet?" The thought struck a disturbing chord. "What

do you suppose I told her? I don't talk to women about my business. All she knows is that I was tried and acquitted."

"You live with her," said Saladin. "Women are curious."

The noise of the children outside became louder. Pelham spoke with despair.

"What do you want me to do? Why don't you tell me?"

"I shall," said Saladin. "And you must listen carefully. This diary is a charge of dynamite. You know this as well as I do. I want it, Pelham. I don't care how you get it, I want it."

Pelham looked at the floor, unwilling to believe what had happened to him. He raised his head.

"I wouldn't even know where to start."

The light still burned in the ceiling. Saladin put it out. "We'll assume that you're telling the truth. Which means that you must start with Raven. You must gain his confidence, tell him that you like this idea of a book. Tell him you're ready to cooperate. You're plausible enough to be able to do this. And remember, your life hangs in the balance."

Saladin pushed Pelham's bag across the table. The Iranian still had the passport and credit cards. The two men walked out to the street. Saladin locked the front door and dropped the keys through the letter-box. The doctor was sitting at the wheel of the Alfa-Romeo wearing his dark glasses. A group of Indian children was playing some game nearby, chanting in Hindi. Pelham slumped down beside Saladin, his bag on his knees. The rules had changed. He had lost control of events. He was only sure of one thing. These people would kill him without compunction.

They recrossed the river. The driver appeared to know exactly where he was going, left onto Old Brompton Road and up Queen's Gate. He turned into a mews with a pub on the corner. Beyond the pub was a cobble-stoned row of garages and houses. The Alfa-Romeo stopped in front of a dirty blue door. The doctor turned and offered his hand to Pelham. Pelham made no move to take it.

"Be polite!" said Saladin. Pelham obeyed.

"The pain will go," the doctor assured him. "There is no need to have the stitches removed. They will disappear."

By the time Saladin opened the blue door, the car had turned and was out of the mews. A steep flight of stairs led to the upper storey. The flat consisted of one room with a bed and a couple of alcoves. There was a shower-stall in one, a small kitchen unit in the other. A cheap clothes-closet, a table, and a couple of chairs completed the furnishing. Blue-checked curtains overlooked the mews.

Saladin pointed at the telephone. "Call your woman!"

"She's not there," Pelham answered. He put his bag on the floor. There was food on the kitchen counter, a refrigerator, and a greasy stove.

"Call her!" Saladin insisted.

The number rang unanswered. Saladin spoke from the window. "Have you got Raven's number?"

Pelham nodded. The card was on the hallway table in Putney but the details were firmly fixed in his mind.

"Say you've had a change of heart," said Saladin. "You'd like to see him now to discuss it."

Pelham redialled. A recorded voice came on the line. "This is John Raven speaking. I'm sorry I'm not here to take your message. If you'll leave your name and address at the tone I'll get back to you. Please speak clearly!"

Pelham cradled the phone. "An answering-machine."

The Iranian came from the window, glancing inside the clothes-closet and opening the drawer in the table.

"Sit down!" He lit a cigarette, looking at Pelham. "You've got to make Raven your friend and you don't have much time to do it."

The Iranian offered the cigarette-pack. Pelham's hand was still trembling.

"I've got to have some sort of story. This man's no fool."

"He's an ex-detective," said Saladin.

What remained of Pelham's courage drained from his body. "You mean you knew this all along!" he protested.

"Ever since Mount told me." The Iranian waved a slim brown hand. "We know people," he added significantly. "Raven's a very cool customer with a reputation for meddling in other people's affairs. And you can be sure of one thing. He won't go anywhere near the police."

The news did nothing to ease Pelham's alarm. "You mean this business about writing a book is a cover?"

Saladin moved a thin shoulder. "It's a possibility. Your job is to convince him. You must stay as close to the truth as you can. Tell him that somebody called you this morning. A stranger. This man spoke about Helga's diary. When you said that you didn't have it, he threatened you. A friend lent you this flat. You don't know what's going on. You're a frightened man."

Pelham dragged deep on his smoke. That much was true. "Why haven't I gone to the police?"

"That is easily answered," Saladin smiled. "You've been through a terrible time. And although your conscience is clear, you're afraid that there could be something in Helga's diary that would land you back in trouble."

The cigarette had become a bitter taste on his tongue and Pelham extinguished it.

"Leave your name on the answering-machine," the Iranian instructed. "Give him this number. And remember, your task is to convince him that you're on his side."

Pelham's good hand roved over the receiver. "What happens to me at the end of all this?"

Saladin smiled. "You stay alive."

"This is Piers Pelham," he said. "Call me on 731-0028. I've got to see you urgently. It's about the diary." He replaced the phone. "What happens now?"

Saladin placed the key to the flat on the table. "You stay here and wait for his call. There's food and something to drink. Don't worry about keeping in touch. We'll always be close."

The street door banged below. Saladin's footsteps sounded on the cobble-stones.

CHAPTER 3

It was a quarter to eight when Raven reached the Lagoon. The bottom half of a warehouse on the river had been turned into a restaurant. The walls were painted with scenes of Venice. The waiters wore red shirts and straw hats with red ribbons. The Thames flowed beneath.

The head waiter bustled forwards. "Good evening, Mister Raven! Your friend is already here. He asked for a table away from the bullshit!" He lifted his hands and smiled.

O'Callaghan was sitting with an array of papers spread out on the table. Raven stuffed them into the lawyer's briefcase.

"I want value for money," he said.

"In that case, I'll have lobster!" The lawyer crossed the room to the fishtank, a dapper figure in a cream suit and navy blue bow-tie. He came back, looking pleased with himself. "I chose the biggest I could find," he announced.

"There's always the chance you could choke on it!" Raven said pleasantly.

He ordered a bottle of Krug, O'Callaghan's favourite. Raven had carp baked in Venetian style. The two men ate without exchanging more than a few words. The waiter cleared the debris and Raven passed an aluminium cylinder across the table. The lawyer sniffed the cigar. "Cuban! God alone knows what this is going to cost me in terms of brain-damage."

He blew out the match and half-closed his eyes as he inhaled. "Don't tell me! Let me guess. If I'm wrong, I'll buy supper. This has got something to do with the German girl."

Raven placed both elbows on the table. "I've seen two people today. The woman where Helga Heumann worked and Pelham. Of him, the less said the better."

O'Callaghan assumed a look of keen interest. "Tell me something, John. What gives you the right to intervene in other people's affairs?"

"I don't need any excuse," Raven answered. "I like to think that I'm moved by a strong sense of lateral justice."

The lawyer closed one eye completely and peered through the cigar smoke.

"What total crap! What happened to the statement that there's no such thing as justice? That it's an abstract concept administered by fallible human beings?"

"OK, then," said Raven. "Let's call it lateral expediency."

The lawyer grinned. "Does that still make you a fallible human being?"

"I try to make allowances for it," said Raven.

The waiter brought coffee and Sambuca. The flames died in the glasses. A coffee-bean floated in each. O'Callaghan played with his spoon.

"There are times when I'm inclined to agree with Kirstie. I sincerely believe that you need some form of psychotherapy." His smile robbed the words of offence.

"I've had it," Raven said shortly. "The people where Helga Heumann worked are called Winebert. Jewish intelligentsia and nice with it! These people really *cared* about Helga, Patrick. The point is, Mrs. Winebert isn't the type to lie. She claims that Helga kept a diary written in German. She actually saw it. You see the implications?"

O'Callaghan sipped his drink reflectively. "Pelham's got it." He said at last.

Raven leaned forward, giving force to his words. "I don't think so, Patrick. In fact I don't think he'd ever heard about it until I told him."

O'Callaghan squinted through the haze of cigar-smoke. "How did he take the news?"

"Badly," said Raven. "I don't mean that he went to pieces

but he definitely tilted. This bastard's guilty, Patrick. I can feel it in my bones. All I need to nail him is that much!" He narrowed a space between thumb and forefinger.

"And where is this diary?"

"I don't know," Raven admitted. "What's important is that it exists."

The lawyer brushed ash from his lapel. "I've done some research of my own, knowing your paranoia about derelict policemen. The two Drugs Squad officers are beyond reproach, boy-scouts with lily-white records. I wouldn't want to see you make a fool of yourself in that direction."

"I don't intend to," said Raven. A couple was being seated at a table nearby. For some reason the woman reminded him of Helga. There was the same look of vulnerability. "I'll tell you what I think," he continued. "Whoever has the diary will have had it translated. And once that's done, they'll know what it's worth."

The lawyer nodded. "I recognize the tone of voice."

Raven let the sally go by without comment. "Helga's arrest was a fluke. More than a million and a half vehicles come through Dover in a year. She had no idea what was in that car when she drove off the ferry. Of course she denied guilty knowledge! She was dead the moment the Drugs Squad arrived. I'm not suggesting that they were bent, Patrick. There *was* no real case against Pelham without her testimony. And she stayed loyal to the prick to the end."

O'Callaghan was at work on his cigar again. "Pelham's guilt is surmisal. The man's been cleared in open court. He may not be the sort of man you introduce to your sister but that's a long way from being a drug-smuggler."

Raven raised his eyebrows. "Really? Then how come he's defended by one of the top Q.C.'s in the country while she gets Legal Aid?"

"I don't know." The lawyer wiped his neat moustache with his napkin. "I have to go. I'm doing duty-solicitor at Horseferry Road in the morning."

Raven paid the bill and they walked outside. The Metro was waiting.

"You want a lift home?" asked Raven.

The lawyer tucked his briefcase under his arm. His cream suit was stained with cigar-ash.

"The air will do me good. Thanks for the meal."

Raven watched him go with affection. Critical, highly intelligent, the lawyer was always there when it mattered. Raven parked in the usual place and went down the steps to the boat. A tracery of lights from the bridge showed on the water beneath. It was barely midnight but no sound came from the other boats. He let himself into the sittingroom, anticipating a little music before he went to bed. Maybe a nightcap. He ran the tape on the answering-machine. Pelham's message came as a total surprise. No answer came when Raven called. He put on an old Peggy Lee record and poured himself a glass of malt. The jangle of the phone burst through the blues. The woman's voice was vaguely familiar.

"Is that Mister Raven?"

"Speaking." It was a quarter to one.

"It's Harriet Horne, Mister Raven. We met this morning, remember? You came to see Piers Pelham and I answered the door." Her voice sounded anxious.

He remembered her well. Her reception had been less than gracious. The memory cooled his enthusiasm.

"Have you any idea at all what the time is?"

"I know," she said quickly. "I'm really sorry. The thing is, I need to talk to you urgently."

"Do it in about twelve hours' time," he suggested. "And go back to bed."

"I haven't *been* to bed," she insisted. "Please don't hang up on me, Mister Raven! *Please!*"

The malt made a warm pool in his stomach. "What's the problem?" he asked.

"Piers hasn't come home."

"He's probably found somewhere better." There was a mild pleasure in bringing her down.

"Don't *be* like that!" she wailed. "I'm in such trouble. The house has been burgled for one thing. I can't call the police. Look, I know why you came to the house. Perhaps I can help you."

Raven sat up straighter. "How would you do that?"

"I can't talk on the phone. I'm too frightened. Look, I'm sitting here petrified! Piers isn't coming back here, Mister Raven. The bastard's walked out on me. The thing is, I know something about his involvement with Helga. Something that nobody else knows."

He was already on his feet, grabbing the car-keys from the top of the desk.

"Lock all the doors and put on every light in the place. I'll be there just as soon as I can!"

The traffic was light and he made good time to Putney. The gate at the end of Pelham's driveway was open. Lights showed through the trees. The front door was thrown open as his tyres crunched gravel. Harriet Horne hurried him into the house.

"Thank God you came!" she said, tears blurring her mascara. The yellow dress deepened her sun-tan.

She caught his hand and pulled him up the stairs. It was a scene that he knew too well from the past. Drawers had been emptied onto the floor, the backs ripped from paintings and photographs. The beds had been left overturned. She looked at him, brushing her eyes.

"Every room is the same!"

He took a turn along the corridor and back. "Have you any idea what's been taken?"

She shook her head. "As far as I can see, nothing. Not that there's much to take. It's a rented house. The television and video are still here. The kitchen looks as though a bomb hit it. The place is knee-deep in flour and sugar. They just emptied the containers where they were standing."

She stayed close to him as they descended the stairs. The

carpets had been yanked from the wainscoting, curtains stripped from the rods. Raven checked the windows and doors. There was no indication of a break-in. A key had been used to obtain entry. He lifted the phone in the hallway. The line was still connected. The card he had given Pelham lay in a tray on the side-table.

"That's how I got your number," she said.

It was the way she said it that decided him. This was a genuinely frightened woman.

"Get your things together," he ordered. "Everything that belongs to you. And hurry!"

She was down in a few minutes, carrying a couple of bags. Raven took them and turned off the lights. He stood in the darkened hallway looking through the window at the side of the door.

"Let's go!" he said. They ran across the gravel. He threw her bags on the back seat.

Her head was bent. She was crying into a handkerchief. He turned the ignition key.

"When did you last see Pelham?"

She looked up, wiping her cheeks. "He left shortly after you did. He said he had some business to take care of. I went to Hurlingham. We were supposed to be spending the evening with friends. He didn't show up or call. It must have been almost midnight when I got back and walked into that!"

She turned her head, looking at the silent house. "I knew," she said bitterly. "I knew as soon as I saw his passport had gone. The bastard walked out on me."

He turned into the avenue and swung left onto a long empty road where lamps shone on deserted pavements. A taxi scooted out of a side-turning. A man and woman were locked in embrace on the passenger-seat.

Her voice was barely audible against the steady hum of the motor. "I don't know how far I can trust you."

"That depends what you're trusting me with," he replied.

She plunged into silence again. Traffic-signals held them at the approach to Putney Bridge. Raven looked sideways at her. The ploy with the police-car had worked. Its presence must have prompted Pelham's quick exit.

A match flared. She spoke with the cigarette in her mouth. "I know the truth about Piers. Anyway, some of the truth. Perhaps we could do a deal."

The signals changed, releasing them. "What would you want in return?"

She thought for a while. "Revenge, I suppose. I don't like being dumped, Mister Raven. Do you want to know where Piers went this morning?"

They were approaching World's End. He took a right at the bend in King's Road.

"I thought he didn't say where he was going."

A streetlamp lit her smile as they neared the Embankment. "He didn't. But a girl like me has to take precautions. He was on the phone in the bedroom. I listened on the downstairs extension."

He pulled into the cul-de-sac. "You can get yourself into trouble that way."

He reached for her bags. "That's my boat over there. There's one thing we have to get straight before you come aboard. This is no time to start lying."

She turned towards him quickly. Her scent seemed part of her body.

"Why do you think I called you, Mister Raven, why?"

He opened his door. "I'm not sure. I'd like you to tell me."

"Because there was nobody else. I'm in trouble and I thought you might help me."

He carried her bags across the Embankment. She was still staying close as they went down the steps. The deck-light was burning. He unlocked the door and put the bags on the floor. She sank down on a couch, looking up at him. He ran the curtains along the rails and went into the kitchen. He took the two cups of coffee into the sittingroom.

She held her cup with both hands. "Piers went to see some-one called Mount. The man said Mount's First Editions."

"Do you have parents?" he asked.

Puzzlement showed in her eyes. "They're divorced. My mother remarried and lives in Portugal. My father's in London. Why do you ask?"

It was a good question and he had no answer except that she seemed lost and lonely like so many of her generation.

"Tell me how you met Pelham," he invited.

She put her cup down on the glass-topped table. "It was the night of his acquittal. Someone Piers was at school with gave a party for him. Piers was the star, of course. Anyway I went home with him to Putney. He'd been drinking a lot of champagne and doing coke. I can't because of my nose. So we went to bed. By this time he was totally out of his head, banging on about the trial and how clever he'd been. I mean it didn't make sense, talking like that to a total stranger. But he didn't seem able to stop. He said that Helga never knew what was in the car, that he'd set up the whole thing with some people. I've never seen anyone as far gone as he was that night. He never referred to it again: I don't think he even remembers what he said."

It was difficult to keep his voice under control. "Did he mention her diary?"

She moved her head from side to side. "After that first time he never spoke about her. He's got no feeling for anyone. He's a monster."

He took her bags into the guestroom and closed the curtains. "This is where you sleep," he said. "The bathroom's next door." He threw a towel on the bed.

She swept her hair back and held it at the back of her neck. Her eyes challenging.

"You don't think much of me, do you?"

He did his best to be honest. "I'm glad that I'm not your father. I'd be sad and very worried."

"Am I allowed to know why?" she asked.

He paused in the doorway. The lighting made her look even younger, more vulnerable.

"Because of the way you live, the people you mix with. Because of the person you are, I suppose. Good night, Harriet. Sleep as long as you can."

He closed the door gently and rang Pelham's number. There was no answer.

CHAPTER 4

Pelham walked up his driveway, hearing the strung-out sound of a hard-hit tennis-ball. He was certain that no one had followed him to Putney. Beech Avenue was empty behind him. The Iranians had taken his house-key but he had to see Harriet. The game had changed since yesterday and he needed her. She wasn't answering the phone but that was typical. Meanwhile he had his excuses ready. He needed her on his side.

He turned the corner into early morning sunshine and stopped dead at the edge of the gravel. There wasn't a window at the front of the house that showed a curtain. He ran up the steps and rang the bell without answer. He lifted the flap on the letter-box and peered into the hallway. White footsteps tracked the dark parquet, coming from the direction of the kitchen. He ran to the back of the house, calling Harriet's name. His voice echoed across the pool. He had a better view of the havoc inside the house from the kitchen window. There were no broken doors, no smashed panes of glass. The implication of an alliance between Harriet and the Iranians jerked his brain into action. He had no doubt what everyone wanted. His only chance in this new game was to stay one long jump ahead. Either way it was the end of a chapter. He had closed a few in his time and survived.

He checked the garage. The Mercedes was still there. The hire bill was long overdue. The repossessmen would be collecting the car any day now. He walked back down the driveway. He'd have to start using buses instead of taxis. An Underground train took him to Hampstead. He walked up the hill, preparing himself for what was certain to be a difficult encounter. Azaleas blazed in the Winebert window-boxes. A Volks-wagen stood outside the house. A woman in rust-coloured linen answered the doorbell. Dark hair framed her handsome face. Her expression changed as she looked at Pelham.

"What do you want?" she demanded.

He stood his ground, realising that she would have seen his picture in the newspapers. He assumed the slightly shamed look that always went well with women.

"How *dare* you come here?" she asked. "Have you no sense of decency at all?"

"I don't think you're doing me justice," he said quietly.

Her expression hardened. "I don't want to talk about justice with you. Now will you please go away?"

"All I want is the chance to be heard," he pleaded.

Mrs. Winebert stood rock-firm against the suggestion. "I don't know how you have the effrontery to come here," she said. "You must know how we felt about Helga."

He came one cautious pace nearer. "That's why I'm here, Mrs. Winebert. To explain. Helga and I never had a real chance. She was already involved with these people when we met. If I'd known the truth then things might have been different."

"Involved?" She spat the word back at him. "That girl could never have done the things they say about her. I don't give a hoot about the verdict. We knew her better. This was her home before you took her away."

Children on ponies trotted up the hill to the heath. He shook his head sadly.

"Before I took her away?" he repeated. I'm sorry, Mrs. Winebert but it wasn't like that. Leaving your home was Helga's idea."

Mrs. Winebert consulted her watch. "I'd rather not continue this conversation."

He raised his good hand in token surrender. "Whatever you say, Mrs. Winebert. But you could tell me at least where she's buried."

She looked surprised at this new dimension. "I've no idea where she's buried. As far as we know, her father has arranged for her body to be taken back to Germany." She was still barring the doorway.

He dragged his eyes from the ground. "I haven't lived a blameless life, I'm the first to admit it. But I'm ashamed of nothing that happened with Helga, Mrs. Winebert. You see I loved her."

"You have a strange way of showing it," she replied.

"The people responsible for her death are the ones who got her into this terrible business in the first place."

She looked him up and down. "Is this another of your play-acting roles? Another piece of fantasy like the farmhouse in Tuscany?"

"The farmhouse could have happened," he insisted. "It's just another instance of us never having had a proper chance. If Helga had told me the truth when we met, we might have worked something out. I know it! And I'm not the only one who thinks so."

She closed the door a few inches, excluding him from her house. "I've no idea what you mean."

"I'm talking about John Raven," he said. "I know he's been here to see you. I'm helping him write a book about the trial. Helga's diary could help us find the answers we're all looking for."

She looked at her watch again. The gesture was pointed. "I have no idea where her diary is, nor do I know what happened to it. Now I'd like you to go, please."

He nodded. "I wish you believed at least some of the things that I've said, Mrs. Winebert. I won't bother you again. Thanks for talking to me."

Pelham took a northbound train from Hampstead to Wimbledon. A traffic-warden showed him the way to the Porlock Riding Stables. Iron gates led to a yard enclosed by loose-boxes. A girl in jeans and green gumboots was hosing the cobbles. She pointed in reply to Pelham's question.

"Through the yard and past the tack-room. You can't miss it."

An old Mustang convertible was parked in front of a Victorian cottage. Curtains blew in the windows. The front door was open.

Pelham rapped a couple of times. "Anyone home?"

A tall man appeared in the hallway wearing a pair of shorts and holed canvas shoes. He had the baked-ochre skin of a man who has lived long in the sun, thinning grey hair and a deeply-lined face.

Pelham offered his hand. "My name is Piers Pelham."

"Gregory Horne." He beckoned Pelham into a chintz-upholstered room with French doors opening onto the garden. Peachtrees were crucified against weathered brick walls. A single croquet hoop spiked the lawn. A mallet and ball lay nearby. A stuffed bear stood in the corner of the sittingroom, attired in a short sequin jacket and a floppy felt hat. There was a golf ball typewriter on the card-table, a piece of paper between the rollers.

Horne came from the kitchen, carrying a jug of Pimm's and two glasses. He filled one and gave it to Pelham.

"You're Harriet's boyfriend, right? I followed the case in the papers. It must have been a very unpleasant experience."

"It still is." Pelham removed the sprig of borage from his glass. "People seem to remember all the wrong things. They remember that I was on trial but they forget the acquittal. It doesn't help in business and it hasn't helped with Harriet."

The older man looked surprised. "I had it in my head that you two met *after* the trial. Or have I got it wrong?"

"No, you're right," said Pelham. "The thing is, when two people have something good going for them there are always others who try to destroy it. That's what's been happening to Harriet and me."

"I'm sorry to hear that," said Horne. "Harriet doesn't confide in me these days but she does call from time to time. I had the idea that she was perfectly happy."

The drink tasted of little but lemonade, but at least it was cool. "I thought so too," answered Pelham. "But it doesn't seem to be like that. I got home last night to find that she'd left. Packed her bags and gone, just like that. I've no idea where she is either. That's why I came to see you."

Horne refilled the glasses. "Did you have a row or what?"

Pelham shook his head. "Not really, no. Things haven't been going too well of late but we've both been under pressure. To tell the truth, I've no idea what brought this on."

"You preach to the converted," smiled Horne. "I've been married three times. Harriet's mother is the last. She's my only child."

Pelham looked through his glass at the garden. "I love Harriet. The problem is that I don't seem to know how to show it. I want to get hold of her before too much harm's done. To be blunt, I want to marry your daughter."

"Then you're a brave man," answered Horne. "I'd better fill you in about my relationship with Harriet. She left this house three years ago. Since then I've seen her on eight occasions, always when she needed something. The last time I spoke to her was a few weeks ago, just after she'd met you. If she's not with you I have no idea where she'd be."

"What about her friends?" asked Pelham.

A water-sprinkler had come to life on the grass outside, creating a rainbow against the sunshine. Horne waved at the far distance.

"Friends?" he repeated doubtfully. "You'd know more about them than I would. She's been sharing flats, living in furnished rooms, ever since she left here. In fact you're the first of her new friends that she's mentioned by name."

Pelham followed the fall of the spray on the lawn. "Would she go to her mother, perhaps?"

"Her mother lives in Estoril," said Horne. "Harriet wouldn't go there. They don't get along. I don't want to sound bitter but Harriet and her mother are much alike in many ways. Harriet has no real feeling for me. She seems to reserve her emotions for people of her own age. She's a manipulator, Piers. I've come to terms with it. If she weren't my daughter, I wouldn't give her another thought."

Pelham looked suitable woebegone. "I didn't mean to upset you," he said. "You can see, I'm not the most tactful person. It's just that I'm desperate to find her before it's too late."

"You're old enough to know what you're doing, I suppose." The self-mocking smile was back on Horne's face. "One possibility comes to mind. There was a girl at Harriet's last school. Emma Murchison. She used to stay here in the past. I imagine that Harriet would still be in touch with her."

"Do you have her address?" Pelham asked quickly.

A frown creased Horne's forehead. "No, I don't, I'm afraid. I suppose we could try the nuns in Ascot. The phone's in my bedroom. You'll find the number in my book."

The page was a record of Harriet Horne's academic progress over the years. Pelham spoke to the bursar.

"I'm trying to get in touch with a girl who was at your school. She left five or six years ago. Her name's Emma Murchison."

The bursar's tone was starched with convent suspicion. "Who exactly is this speaking?"

"Piers Pelham, a friend of Gregory Horne. Emma used to stay with him."

"One moment, please!" It was five minutes before the woman was back on the line. "Would that be Harriet Horne's father?"

"That's right."

"I'm afraid I can't help you," the woman said. "The only address we have is of Emma's guardian and he died three years ago."

"No luck," Pelham announced, coming back into the sunny sittingroom. "They only had the address of Emma's guardian and he's dead."

"Christ, so he is!" said Horne. "Hanged himself from a tree in the garden, poor bugger. Children have a lot to answer for."

Pelham looked blank.

"Hector Reynolds," said Horne. "Emma was the daughter he wanted and never had. Her own parents died when she was eleven. She didn't treat Hector too well."

Pelham scribbled on a piece of paper and gave it to Horne. "This is the number where I'm staying. If Harriet should get in touch with you, please ask her to contact me. Tell her Putney's not the same without her."

He left the cottage, displaying bravery in face of discouragement. He was on the lane before he realised that he had no audience.

Raven answered the phone. He recognised Pelham's voice immediately.

"I left my phone off the hook last night," said Pelham. "When can we meet?"

"You'll have to do better than that," said Raven. He was in the sittingroom, still in his robe. It was almost noon but no sound came from Harriet's bedroom. "What about the diary?"

"All hell's broken loose," said Pelham. "Look, I *have* to see you! I'm coming with my tail between my legs. Just give me a time and a place."

"You still haven't answered my question," Raven pointed out.

"I don't want to talk about it over the phone."

Raven looked over his shoulder. The bathroom door closed. "Do you know where Oakley Street is? It runs south from King's Road to Battersea Bridge."

"Got it," said Pelham.

"Turn right at the bottom," Raven instructed. "You'll see some houseboats moored on the left. Mine is the first coming from the bridge. The *Albatross*. There's an entryphone at the bottom of the steps. Be there at two o'clock."

"I'll be there," Pelham promised.

Raven found a clean pair of jeans and a shirt and dressed hurriedly. He tapped on Harriet's door.

"That was your boyfriend on the phone. He'll be here at two o'clock!"

She opened the door, naked from the waist up, her long dark hair cascading over her shoulders. There was no disloyalty in the thought that her breasts were smaller and firmer than Kirstie's. He had cheated twice on his wife and regretted both occasions.

Harriet Horne pulled her dress over her head and walked past him into the kitchen. He switched on the percolator and went out on deck. It was the twentieth day of uninterrupted sunshine in the southeast corner of England. There was relief in the promise that rain would come soon. Raven watered the roses and hosed down the deck, aiming the final burst at a gull perched on the television mast. His mental sights were fixed upon Pelham. The man was plausible, cunning, and pitiless. Whatever he said was to be disbelieved.

Hank Lauterbach was sitting under a makeshift awning, a fishing line tied to his bare leg, the float drifting a few yards downstream. Raven had never known his friend to catch anything. The Great Dane's tail semaphored welcome as Raven came on deck.

Lauterbach was not much given to smiling. It was all the more engaging when he did.

"I saw the face at the window," he said. "Congratulations!"

Raven perched his buttocks on the rail. "A lady in trouble."

Lauterbach scratched his head through the knotted handkerchief he was wearing.

"You may rely on my discretion."

"Some very unpleasant people are giving her problems," said Raven. "Pelham is one of them. He'll be here at two o'clock. I want you to keep her on your boat until he's gone."

"Sure," said his friend. "She may not think much of the quarters."

"She'll do what she's told," Raven replied. "I'll bring her across as soon as she's had her coffee. If she asks any questions you don't know the answers."

"Will do!" Lauterbach stretched his legs, releasing a cloud of greyish powder where he had been sandpapering the bottoms of his calloused feet.

Raven came off the rail. "And if she wants to talk about the trial, you don't know anything about that either."

Harriet had poured the coffee and tied her hair with a scarlet ribbon. Silver hoops in her ears gave her the look of a gypsy.

She spooned marmalade onto her toast as he sat down, facing her.

"Did you hear what I said before?" he demanded. "Pelham will be here at two o'clock."

She spoke with her mouth full. "You don't believe me, do you! I mean about him being drunk and saying those things?"

"I believe you," said Raven. "Let's hope that he doesn't remember. Get your things together. I'm taking you across to another boat. I want you to stay there until I come to collect you. And I mean stay below, out of sight."

She eyed him over the coffee-bowl. "I feel safe enough here."

"You're not," he told her. "Try to think of somewhere to stay. Somewhere out of London."

She wiped her mouth and fetched her bags from the guest-room. "Just what *have* I got myself into, Mister Raven?"

"You're growing up," he said.

He escorted her across the gangway and introduced her to Lauterbach. "Keep an eye on her," said Raven.

The American made a circle with thumb and forefinger. "As safe as a vestal virgin!"

Pelham leaned on the stone parapet looking down at the boats. The *Albatross* nuzzled the fenders, a broad-beamed barge with rose-bushes growing in tubs on the deck. A cedarwood superstructure covered two-thirds of the deck. Pelham craned out farther. A bead curtain hung in the doorway. It was impossible to see through the windows. A network of makeshift gangways connected the rest of the motley craft.

He made his way down the stone steps and spoke into the entryphone. The door clicked open. Raven was waiting beyond the bead curtain. Pelham looked at him covertly. The long, greying hair was cut modishly. The tall man was wearing tie-dyed jeans, a red gingham shirt, and sneakers.

Raven pointed at a couch and Pelham sat down. Wrap-around windows allowed a view of the river and bridges in both directions. The room reflected the tastes of its owner. The antique desk looked like a collector's piece. A Bang & Olufsen music-centre fitted into an alcove. Pride of place was given to a small abstract painting hanging on the end wall. The mixture of high-tech and respect for the past increased Pelham's uneasiness.

Raven's eyes were blue, clear, and vigilant and fixed upon Pelham's left hand. Pelham lifted it indifferently.

"An accident yesterday. I caught it in a cab door." He grinned at his own clumsiness.

Raven took the chair by his desk and stretched out long legs. He was wearing no socks. He waited for Pelham to continue. The kitchen door swung with the movement of the boat. Pelham could see the bathroom at the end of the short corridor.

His nervousness was unfeigned. "Are we alone?"

"We're alone," Raven said easily. "I tried your number last night."

Pelham reached for a cigarette. "I'm afraid I didn't put the phone back properly. I only discovered it this morning. Has Harriet Horne been in touch with you? The girl you saw at my place."

Raven moved his head from side to side. "No, why should she? I don't even know the woman."

"That wouldn't stop her," said Pelham. "We had an argument yesterday morning. God only knows what about. I can't even remember. I suppose the truth is that I've been pretty uptight since the trial finished. You know, trying to get my life in some sort of order?"

"I thought you came here to talk about Helga," said Raven.

"Can I do it my own way?" asked Pelham. "One thing's tied up with another."

"Take your time," Raven said.

"I was out all day," said Pelham. "I must have called Harriet half a dozen times. No reply. I didn't think much of it—she's a sulker. Anyway, I got home just after midnight. No Harriet, no note. Nothing. I'd been there about twenty minutes or so when I heard this noise on the gravel outside. I assumed it was her and opened the front door. Is there any chance of a drink?"

He watched Raven into the kitchen. Sunshine flooded the corridor. Raven returned with a can of Foster's. Pelham opened his throat to the cool lager.

He placed the empty can on the table beside him. "Two men were standing on the doorstep. One of them had a gun. They were in like a flash and I found myself on a chair with the gun at the back of my head. They started banging on about Helga's diary. I knew where it was, they said. If I didn't produce it, they'd kill me."

Raven wiped his mouth with the back of his hand. "Just keep the narrative flowing and don't stray too far from the facts."

"They started asking about Harriet," Pelham said. "How long had we lived together? Where was she now? Had she been a friend of Helga's?"

Raven blew smoke at the ceiling. "And you think they were somehow connected with Helga. Is that what you're saying?"

"What else?" Pelham shrugged. "They knew all about the trial. They were Arabs of some kind, Iranians, maybe. The one doing most of the talking said they had friends in the police and they'd know if I lodged a complaint. I could run, they said, but they'd always be able to find me."

"And you took all this seriously?" Raven looked fascinated.

Pelham grinned ruefully. "Wouldn't you? My worry was Harriet. I thought of her walking in on all that . . ." He shook his head, staring at the floor. "They were there for almost an hour, tearing the place apart. They'd be in touch, they said, then they left just like that."

"And still no sign of Harriet?" Raven asked.

Pelham lifted his chin. "Not a peep. Thank God for her sake! But her things were gone when I looked in the bedroom. I got out of there fast. A friend lent me a flat in Queen's Gate. That's the number I gave you."

It was thin in patches, he thought, but plausible. He was totally unprepared for Raven's next question.

"Who paid for your defence?"

Pelham assumed a look of regret. "Touché," he said. "I know what you're going to think. I'm not a lot of good to anyone and you're right. My mother cashed in a life-insurance policy."

The confession had no visible effect upon Raven. "I still don't understand why you're here. What does it have to do with me?"

Pelham spoke with sincerity. "Everyone wants Helga's diary. I just follow the money."

"You mean you know where the diary is?"

"No I don't," Pelham admitted. "But if anyone can find it, I can."

Raven was watching a man with a dog on the neighbouring boat. "You could be on dangerous ground," Raven said quietly. "Do you still think that Helga was guilty?"

Pelham achieved what he hoped was a look of frankness. "It speaks for itself, surely! She was a kid who got in completely out of her depth and I'm sorry for her. I'd like to help you put the record straight."

"Bullshit!" Raven said pleasantly.

"What do you mean?" Pelham said. "These people are scared of whatever Helga wrote in her diary and I was her boyfriend. It's as simple as that."

Raven's eyes were blue lasers. "Shall I tell you what I think?" he said. "I think you're a self-dedicated bastard who is incapable of performing one single unselfish act."

"You're wrong," Pelham said quickly. "You're wrong about Helga and you're wrong about me."

There was no sign of Raven retracting his statement. "No. I'm right and you know it. You say that you feel you're in danger. OK. But these people can only kill you. I'm the one you have to worry about."

Pelham slipped into his next role with the skill of a quick-study actor.

"OK, I've lied to you. But there was a reason." He lifted his left hand. "Those people did come to the house that night. And this was no accident! They took me to this place in South London. I was *supposed* to come here and pretend to cooperate with you! These people are crazy, Raven. Nobody's safe while the diary's missing. They had this notion that Helga had left it in the house, that Harriet might have found it."

"How did my name come up?" Raven's eyes never left Pelham's face.

"I told them everything," Pelham admitted, feeling on firmer ground.

"Where are you staying?"

"Twenty-four-A Queen's Gate Mews." Pelham made a gesture of hopelessness. "You've got the telephone number."

Raven walked to the end of the room and stared through the window. He swung round behind outstretched finger.

"You're a worthless bastard. Your life, your thinking, all of it worthless. You may not realise this, but I'm your only chance of survival. I'm going to take a calculated risk with you. I intend to nail these people and you're going to be the bait!"

"I'm on your side anyway," said Pelham.

"You're on nobody's side but your own," replied Raven. "You've got one way to go. Make your friends happy. Tell them you've got me conned. Say that I think you're going to help me find Helga's diary. It's your only chance of survival. Either that or go to the police."

Pelham came to his feet. "I told you, I need the money. I've got to get out of this country. I'll do what you said."

Raven parted the bead curtain and glanced up at the Embankment. "You realise that you'll be watched?"

"I'm keeping my eyes open." Pelham stepped out on deck.
"You wouldn't know," Raven answered. "Get on back
where you live and leave that phone on the hook. "You'll be
hearing from me."

CHAPTER 5

It was an hour since Pelham had left the boat, and Harriet was back on the *Albatross*. When Raven came from the bathroom she was sitting on the couch with her shoes on the floor beside her. Sunshine pierced the bead curtain throwing a pattern on the wall. Something about the way Harriet looked at him made him glance at his desk. His address-book was lying on top. In it was Pelham's new telephone number. Instinct told Raven that Harriet had opened the book while he had been out of the room.

"I can't *believe* this!" she said, meeting his gaze. "What does he want from me?"

Raven sat down beside her. "His friends think that you know where Helga's diary is."

"That's ridiculous," she cried. "I never even heard of it until I met you."

He slipped the address-book into his pocket. "Pain can screw up a man's thinking. They chopped the top off one of his fingers."

She covered her mouth with a hand, her eyes shocked. "My God!"

"The idea probably made some sort of sense," said Raven. "While they're looking for you they're not worrying about him."

She made a sound of disgust. "He can drop dead as far as I'm concerned."

To Raven it seemed overdone, as if she were trying to convince him. The truth was that Pelham and she were two of a kind. They were both totally self-centred.

Harriet swung her legs off the sofa and slipped her feet into her shoes. Her eyes were questioning.

"Do you think I should go to the police?"

"What would you tell them?" he asked. "That Pelham got drunk and confessed to you? The man's been tried and acquitted. Believe me, I *know* what goes on inside a police-station. The line forms on the right, women with grudges. Wives, girl-friends, mothers sometimes. All trying to put some guy behind bars. You'd get one of those old sergeants with silver hair, nearing retirement. He'd give you ten minutes and a cup of tea and show you the door. And who'd be waiting outside, Pelham!"

She traced the outline of her lips with the tip of a finger. "Do you think that Piers would really kill me, Mister Raven?"

"A man in fear of his own life will do most things." He reached for the cigarette-pack.

She lit the Gitane for him. "He might if he remembered what he told me."

"That's why we need to play for time, put you somewhere safe where none of these people can get at you."

She shivered theatrically, then seemed to catch fire. "Hey, I've just had a brilliant idea. I was at school with someone called Emma Murchison and we're still pretty close. She restores china and lives by herself down in Somerset."

He placed the phone in her lap. "Tell her you need a bed. Ask if you can come down tonight. Don't tell her the real reason."

She smiled at him as she talked almost provocatively. He was sure now that she'd looked in his address-book.

"Emma?" she said. "It's me, Harriet! Look, can you give me a bed for a couple of weeks? No, I mean *now,* today! No, I'm not in trouble, just thoroughly miserable. Of *course,* it's a man, what else?"

She cupped her hand over the mouthpiece. "She'll pick me up at Sherborne Station. There's a train from Waterloo that gets in at ten past five."

"Tell her a friend is driving you down!" Raven instructed. "You'll be there sometime between five and six."

She relayed the message and put the phone back on the desk. "She understands. She's been through all this herself."

He picked up his car-keys and walked to the bead curtain. "I'll be back in a couple of minutes."

Lauterbach was taking a piece of dog meat from the end of his fishing-line.

"Even this doesn't work," he said with disgust.

"I'm driving the lady down to the country," said Raven.

Lauterbach nodded morosely. "Some people have all the luck."

"I'm coming straight back," said Raven. "Keep an eye on the boat."

Harriet was standing with her bags near the end of the gangway. Raven switched on the answering-machine and locked up behind him. They crossed to the cul-de-sac. The Metro put him in mind of his wife. Write a book, she suggested. He wondered how she'd react to the introduction of Harriet Horne into the cast of characters.

He opened the sun-roof and waited to filter into the westbound traffic. Signals changed at the end of the bridge. Raven slid the car into the wake of a milk-truck registered in Wincanton. Its bulk would serve as a shield until they reached the motorway. Sun flashed from the windshields of oncoming vehicles. His body felt as if it were dissolving under the flimsy shirt. Harriet reached across and pulled down his sun-visor. The upper part of her arm touched his cheek.

"Those pictures on the boat," she said. "Are they of your wife?"

"Yes." He was watching a grey Mazda in the rearview mirror. "Yes, all of my wife."

She swung one of the hooped earrings on her finger. "She's very attractive."

"Attractive and very astute."

He braked suddenly, swerving into a service station. He

checked the pressure in his tyres, watching the Mazda go by. It had disappeared by the time Raven reached the Chiswick flyover. Once on the motorway, he moved into the fast lane. They made good time, Harriet acting as pilot. They turned off at the Wincanton exit, then left towards Templecombe. A lane ran between tall hawthorn hedgerows. Electrified-wire fenced in paddocks where brood-mares were grazing. They passed a fieldstone farmhouse. A Labrador dozed in the evening sunshine.

Harriet Horne straightened up. "After the next bend!" She looked at herself in the mirror on the back of her sun-visor. The hedge broke on the right. An old hunter and a donkey hung their heads over a gate. The cottage was built of the same fieldstone as the farmhouse. The front door opened onto the lane. A Range-Rover was parked in a carport at the side. A girl in a paint-smeared smock came to meet them. The two women threw their arms around one another. Harriet made the introductions.

Emma Murchison had the prettiness that coarsens with middle age, red hair and eyes the colour of an Algarvean lizard. Her smile was engaging.

"Come on into the house!" She took Harriet's bags.

The hallway was cheerful with Lucy Atwell drawings. A wall had been ripped out at the back, turning kitchen and parlour into one large room with comfortable country furniture and a bank of modern kitchen-equipment. Raven perched himself on a window-seat. A couple of magpies flapped off the grass. A pine studio with many windows had been built at the end of the garden. There was a china pig on the sill. Raven lifted it gingerly.

Emma smiled from the gas-stove. "There's a story attached to that animal. A boyfriend bought it for me six years ago. He dropped it on the way to my flat and arrived with a bag full of pieces. He was so upset that I bought some Eponyx and stuck it together. There were *fourteen* separate pieces! The boyfriend has gone long ago but I'll always be grateful to him. He started me on china restoration."

He inspected the glaze and detected no sign of a join. "Magic," he said and replaced it.

"I keep it for sentimental reasons." She carried a tray across with tea and a plate of scones. "I get these locally." She put the tray on the window-seat beside him. Cup and saucer were of wafer-thin porcelain with borders of flying swifts. He spooned damson preserve onto a scone. Harriet was moving about upstairs.

Emma drank, holding her cup with both hands, looking at Raven. "Are you a new friend or an old friend of Harriet's?"

"New," he said. "But not that kind of friend." He let it go at that.

Her expression was regretful. "She hasn't had a lot of luck with men. Did you know the last one?"

"I have to be getting back," he said, rising as Harriet appeared on the stairs. "I'm glad to have met you, Emma. Thanks for the tea."

Harriet walked out to the car with him. "You're as safe here as you'll ever be," he said to her. "Just don't do anything stupid. I'll call you tomorrow."

She reached up on her toes and kissed him on the lips. "Thank you for all that you've done for me. I promise I won't let you down."

She was still waving as he turned into the bend. It was easy driving, returning to London. Most of the traffic was travelling in the opposite direction. Raven drove with his thoughts fixed on Pelham. He wondered what Harriet could have seen in him. The man had the charm and compassion of a cobra.

There were two messages on his answering-machine. Both were from Kirstie. The second was sharper in tone than the first. He called the hotel in Vienna and managed to catch her dressing for supper. He could hear the drone of the hairdryer in the background.

"Where on earth have you been?" she demanded. "I've been trying to reach you for hours!"

"Out!" he said, taking the phone to the couch. "I've been doing research for the book."

The noise of the hairdryer decreased in volume. "What book?" she asked.

"The book you're always saying I should write," he replied.

"Fantastic," she said. "What's it about?"

"The trial."

Her tone changed abruptly. "You mean with all your experiences, you have to pick on a sordid subject like that?"

"I've got a vested interest," he said. It was a battle that had to be fought but was better delayed. "What did you call me for?"

"Well, for one thing to see if I still had a husband," she said. "Did you water the rose-bushes?"

"Twice a day," he said. The room still smelled of Harriet's scent. "And I collected your dry-cleaning. A very exciting programme. Was there anything else?"

"I don't like your tone," she said tartly. The hairdryer stopped. "About this book, are you sure it's a good idea? I mean what about libel? Have you talked to Patrick about it?"

"I had supper with him last night. He thinks it's a good idea." The oval mirror gave him a glimpse of himself, smiling.

"Then he's as daft as you are," his wife said. "It's pathetic, as soon as I'm out of the country you're wallowing in all the old horrors."

"And without even asking permission!"

"*Permission!*" She made a bad word of it. "Since when did you ever ask permission for anything? I'm talking about plain common sense. I worry about you when I'm not there."

"I'll be at Heathrow on Tuesday," he said, reading the note he had made. "OS 451, ten twenty-five."

Her laugh told him that he was forgiven. "By the way, Scherz have come up with an offer. They want me to photograph murals. Political murals, protest murals. Pornography.

Anywhere people find walls and make statements. It could be interesting."

"Terrific," he said. "I'll see you on Tuesday. Love you!"

He walked across to the neighbouring boat. Lauterbach looked up, nodding across at the mud-flats on the south bank. A boy with a baseball cap was fishing from an upturned milk-crate.

"See that little bastard? He caught two fish while I was carving my goddam corns."

"Get him to give you lessons," said Raven. "Did anything happen while I was away? Anyone hanging around?"

"Nothing," said Lauterbach. He reeled in his line and shook his fist at the boy. The boy stuck two fingers in the air and continued to fish.

"I just spoke to Kirstie," Raven said. "I mentioned the book. She wasn't exactly in favour of it. Ah well, she'll come around, no doubt."

Lauterbach wiped his feet on a grimy towel and pushed up his spectacles.

"You know, you've got a serious problem, my friend. You really believe all this shit, I mean *really* believe it! You've got a beautiful wife, enough money to live like a prince yet you still go off on these highs. I just don't understand you."

"Let me ask you a question," said Raven. "Don't you ever have the need to do something that you know to be right?"

"I shun it," Lauterbach said righteously. "That kind of stuff gets me in serious trouble."

Raven smiled. "We all do our own thing. The trick is to do it and think about the reasons afterwards. That's if it makes you feel better."

It was peaceful aboard his own boat. Harriet had tidied her bed and washed the ashtrays. He lifted the phone on impulse and called Somerset. Emma Murchison answered.

"John Raven," he said. "May I have a word with Harriet?"

She came on the line, "You got home all right?"

"No problems," he said. "How are things with you?"

"Fine," she replied. "We've been sitting here, talking about men. Just gossiping, really."

"Good," he said. "I was just checking. I'll call you tomorrow. And don't forget your promise."

"Which promise was that?"

"That you wouldn't do anything stupid."

She was quiet for a few seconds, then she laughed. "Know something, Mister Raven? You're cool. Too cool to be a girl's father!"

Pelham climbed the stairs and inspected the lock on the door at the top. The piece of lint he had pushed into the keyhole was undisturbed. No one had been in the flat during his absence. The sun had set, taking the heat of the day, but it was still too warm for a jacket. He ate in a pizzeria in Harrington Gardens, watchful of people he passed in the street. It was after eight when he made his way home. The phone rang almost immediately. Harriet Horne's voice came as a complete surprise.

"Hi!" he said, smiling into the mouthpiece. "Where are you, for God's sake?"

"I'm where you can't get at me." She sounded edgy but confident. "Were you getting worried?"

His brain shifted a gear. He had to keep this dialogue going. "I'm not sure what that's supposed to mean," he said.

"Well for one thing I've walked out on you. The woman who knew too much, remember?"

"Listen," he said very calmly. "Where did you get this number?"

"Someone I know gave it to me. How's your poor finger?"

His voice sank to an urgent plea. "I've got to see you, Harriet. I'm in serious trouble and need your help."

Her laugh was scornful. "You need *my* help!"

"That's right," he insisted. "We need each other. Why didn't you come home? Have you any idea what happened?"

"Yes," she replied. "I left because I don't like the business you're in or the people you mix with, Piers. You've got a bad memory, darling. You forget things you say."

A chill crept into his consciousness. He searched the dark corners of his mind. The memory formed slowly at first then with complete clarity.

"There's someone at the door," he said quickly. "Call me back in five minutes! Collect, remember! That way I'll know that it's you."

He replaced the phone and drank a glass of water. His hands were unsteady. He turned his wrist, watching the sweep of the second hand on his watch. A nightmare had become a reality. The phone came to life.

"Are you 01-279-8461?"

He cleared his throat. "That's right."

"I have a collect call for you from Somerset. Will you accept?"

"Not unless I know who is calling."

The operator's voice sounded bored. "The name of the subscriber is Emma Murchison and the number is 09-632-8615."

"I'll take it," he said.

The line clicked and the operator was back. "I'm afraid you have lost your connection, caller. The receiver has been replaced at the other end."

Pelham felt for the chair. The line must have been left open. Harriet had heard his conversation with the operator. He waited for a couple of minutes, dialled Directory Enquiries and turned on the charm.

"Good evening. This is Doctor Hendry speaking. Look, I have a small problem! I've just had the results of some tests that were made on a patient who is on holiday. It's very important that the results are at her home when she gets back. What's happened is that my secretary has lost the patient's address. All we have left is the telephone number. Can you help?

"If you'll give the name and number, caller."

"Emma Murchison. 09-632-8615." He waited with pen poised above paper.

The answer came promptly, new-style British Telecom service, brisk and efficient.

"The address is Fox Cottage, Horsington, Templecombe."

Pelham swung the dial again. Mount's hoarse rasp responded.

"Tell them I need to see them," said Pelham. "I don't give a shit," he said, cutting through the objections. "Just give them the message. I need to see someone *now!*"

He sluiced his face with cold water. The glove-stall had not been removed. The finger was sore but there was no fresh bleeding. He planted a chair by the window and sat watching the street. Half an hour went by before the Alfa-Romeo turned into the mews. The front door opened below. Footsteps sounded on the stairs. Pelham came to his feet as Saladin came into the room, his right hand hidden in his jacket pocket.

Twilight made the Iranian's face difficult to discern. His tone was suspicious.

"Why are you in the dark?"

"I wanted to be sure," said Pelham. He crossed the room and sat on the bed.

The light came on. "You were told not to call Mount," said Saladin.

"Harriet Horne called. She knows about Helga and me."

The gun pointed at Pelham. The eyes behind it were as dead as a snake's.

"It was when we first met," said Pelham. "I was drunk. I can't remember exactly what I said. But Harriet knows."

Saladin spat full in his face. "You piece of shit! I should have got rid of you months ago. How did the woman get this number?"

Pelham wiped the spittle from his cheek. "It must have come from Raven."

"You said nothing about this yesterday." Saladin dragged the curtain across the window.

"Harriet could have called him." Pelham was floundering. "She went to the country." He proffered the piece of paper with the address.

Saladin took it. His anger seemed to have subsided. "When are you seeing Raven again?"

"He said he'd call me tomorrow. He's giving me money to work with him. He trusts me."

The Iranian's mouth was contemptuous. "He trusts you as much as I do. But that doesn't matter. The important thing is for you to stay close to him. We'll do the rest."

He unfastened the door and paused at the top of the stairs. "No more calls to Mount and no more calls to the girl!"

CHAPTER 6

Saladin left his apartment through the back entrance, emerging onto Queen's Gate. Reza was outside Imperial College at the wheel of the rented Mercedes 220. Saladin clipped on his seatbelt. It was almost ten by the clock on the dashboard. He spread the survey map on his knees. Pockets sagged in his cotton jacket.

"How long will the journey take?"

Reza turned the ignition key and listened to the sound of the motor.

"It will depend on the traffic. An hour and a half at most."

Saladin's finger traced their route on the map. Their destination lay on the Somerset-Dorset border.

"Pelham may well have talked to others," he said.

Reza brooded behind his dark glasses. "I don't know why the mongrel is living. Much better to make a clean sweep of it."

"For the moment we need him." Saladin glanced away through the window.

They were in the main stream of traffic, travelling west. The hire-car had a good turn of foot. Saladin checked the clip in the .38 and dropped the gun in his baggy jacket.

"What did they say at the Clinic?"

Reza's eyes followed the beam of his headlamps. "They have given me two weeks leave of absence. No problem."

The milestones flashed by, the ribbon of road chasing the last of the daylight. It was dark by the time they turned off at Wincanton. Saladin held the map under the dashboard light.

"Second on the right," he instructed.

They ghosted down a narrow lane. A farmhouse loomed on

the right then a cottage with a Range-Rover under a carport. The curtains were open. Two women were sitting in front of a television set. Neither turned as the car passed. A rough track went to a barn in an oat-stubble field. The Mercedes jolted in beside bales of straw. They were a hundred yards from the cottage. The two men donned gloves and walked back down the lane. The night smelled slightly of pepper. The sliver of moon was tipped on its back. They walked in silence, casting no shadows, approaching the cottage by way of the carport. A horse coughed in the darkness. Light streamed across the grass at the rear of the house, reflected in the studio windows. Saladin flattened his shoulders against the rough stone and inched towards the kitchen window. Reza followed. They had a foreshortened view of the scene inside. A red-headed woman wearing shorts and a man's shirt was brushing her hair as she watched the programme. Saladin recognised the brunette from the pictures that had been taken of her with Pelham. A box of chocolates lay on the table between the two women.

Saladin signalled Reza forwards. They ducked low and ran past the window. Saladin turned the handle of the back door. They burst into the room before either woman knew what was happening. The redhead's face froze in fear as she saw the automatic pistol in Saladin's hand. Reza kicked the door shut and produced a hypodermic syringe from his pocket. Saladin held the women at bay with the gun as Reza sank the hypodermic needle into the neck of an ampoule. He squirted a few drops of liquid into the air and plunged the needle into the fleshy part of the redhead's arm. She had time to scream once before the Pentothol took effect. She slipped to the floor on her buttocks and pitched sideways.

Reza turned sharply as Harriet Horne lashed out with her foot. The kick caught Reza low on the thigh. He grunted with pain.

Saladin clipped the back of her head with his gun. She collapsed in the chair, covering her head with her arms. She offered no resistance as Reza injected her arm. She slumped, her head hanging low on her chest, arms dangling. The brawl had wrenched the jackplug from the wall, silencing the television and extinguishing a couple of bracket-lamps. Reza stuck the plug back in the socket.

Neither man spoke. Each knew what he had to do. They searched the house comprehensively, replacing any object that had been moved. Saladin ensured that the upstairs windows were closed. The Iranians came down the stairs. Emma Murchison lay on the floor snoring heavily. Spittle dribbled from Harriet Horne's mouth. Saladin shut all remaining windows and locked the back door from inside. Then he opened the gas-oven and turned on the burners. They left the house through the front door, standing under the porch as gas crept through the cottage. Not a sound came from the lane. Saladin lifted the flap on the letter-box. The smell of gas was much stronger. He took the roll of Petrex from his pocket and poked the free end of the fuse through the flap. He fed in a few more feet and started to walk towards the Mercedes, unwinding the reel of fuse as he went. Petrex burned at the rate of six inches a minute. Combustion left a faint trail of grey powder that was dispersed by the first breath of air. Saladin lit the end of the fuse. Both men sprinted for the barn. They were four miles away when they heard the explosion. The car windows rattled in sympathy. They stopped in a lay-by near Stonehenge. Moonlight embellished the ancient ruins. Saladin rezipped his trousers and walked back to the car. Reza was watching him through the open window.

"Where is the rope?" asked Saladin.

Reza gave him the car-keys. "In the trunk."

The twelve-feet length of nylon sash-cord was wrapped in a plastic cover. Saladin took out the cord and dropped the cover in a nearby refuse bin. The cord made a compact coil in his pocket. He climbed back into the car. They were in London shortly after midnight. The car-hire office was closed. Reza drove the Mercedes onto the forecourt, locked it, and left the keys in the tailpipe. A taxi ferried them to Leicester Square.

Night-hawks quartered the streets. Window-shoppers, hustlers, the troubled in spirit. The two men waited their turn at the bank of telephone booths. There were no doors on the booths and the babble was loud. Saladin moved as a place became vacant. It took some time before Mount answered.

"I'll be there in five minutes," said Saladin and put the phone down.

Cecil Court was a walkway between Charing Cross Road and Saint Martin's Lane. The shops specialised in second-hand books, prints, military memorabilia, and ballet-shoes. The legend MOUNT'S FIRST EDITIONS was inscribed on the window. The light upstairs was the only one showing in the Court. Saladin rang the doorbell. The curtain moved overhead. They heard footsteps, Mount struggling with the chain. Then the door opened. They stepped inside quickly. The bookdealer was wearing a grey flannel robe over his pajamas and slippers. He looked from Saladin to Reza, his face uncertain. A plume of thin hair rose from the back of his head.

"Come," said Saladin. "We'll talk upstairs."

They climbed to an airless room with heavy Victorian furniture and dark somber paintings. A pile of catalogues ready for posting stood in a table. A dusty chandelier hung from a bolt inserted into the ceiling. The door to the bedroom was open. A reading-lamp shone at the head of the bed. Saladin lowered the venetian blind. Mount watched bewildered as Saladin climbed onto the table and looped one end of the sash-cord over the hook attached to the bolt. He tested his weight on the cord with both hands and jumped down.

"You must have fortitude," he said, producing the gun from his pocket.

Mount's eyes fastened on the two men's gloved hands. He came to life suddenly, losing both slippers in an attempt to reach the top of the stairs. They dragged him back, ashen-faced, his scream barely audible. He wriggled desperately as Reza slipped the noose over his head. He tried to sit down on the floor, finding his voice again. They lifted him bodily onto the table. Saladin jerked the table away. Mount's body dropped like a sack of potatoes, his feet only inches away from the floor. The chandelier swayed, plaster flaking from the ceiling. The sash-cord dug deeply into Mount's scraggy neck. He danced in the air, gurgling and trying to reach the cord with his hands.

Saladin walked into the bedroom. The book Mount had been reading lay on the bed, his place held with his spectacles. Saladin slipped them back in their case and returned the book to the shelf. A choking noise was coming from the other room. He opened the cupboard and took out the folder inside. He emptied the contents onto the floor. They lay in a heap, letters from the Royal Marsden Hospital and a Bavarian clinic, a sheaf of X-ray pictures.

Reza stepped away from Mount's limp body as Saladin walked back into the sittingroom. Mount's false teeth had fallen out, leaving his face collapsed. The bookdealer's eyes bulged and there was a smell of excrement. Saladin tipped the table on its side.

Reza wiped his gloved hands on Mount's flannel robe. "He's dead," he said.

Saladin took one last look round the room. He extinguished the light on the stairs and stationed himself at a first-floor window. When the walkway was clear outside, he opened the door. The two men walked off in opposite directions.

Raven was slightly drunk when he left Meridiana. A cab took him back to the boat. He stood at the top of the steps, looking down at the barge floating in stately fashion, its hull silvered by moonlight. Strains of "Pale Hands I Loved" drifted across the water, sung in an uneasy baritone. The Commander was entertaining. Raven let himself in. The big room had borrowed the smell of the roses outside. He switched on the answering-machine. Harriet Horne's voice spoke to him.

"Please call me the moment you're home! It's very, very important!"

He dialled immediately, recognising the urgency in her

voice. He waited some time for an answer but the line was lifeless. He tried again without success. He got through to the operator.

"No answer you say? If you'll give me the number I'll try to connect you."

She was back in less than a minute. "The number you requested is temporarily out of order."

"How could that be?" he argued. "I've got a message from these people on my answering-machine."

Her voice took on the weariness of someone who has answered the same sort of question too many times.

"These things have to start somewhere, sir. I'll see that it's reported to the engineers. Please try again in the morning!"

Raven slept fitfully and was glad when the night was over. He reached for the phone. Emma Murchison's number was still not replying. It was a quarter of eight and light outside. He called the engineers, asked to speak to a supervisor and explained his predicament. The call was returned within minutes.

"The number in question has been taken out of service, sir. I'm sorry but that is the only information we have. I can only tell you what comes up on the screen. Try again later during the day."

Raven swung himself out of bed and padded into the kitchen. He drew the curtain, set the percolator going, and dropped a slice of bread in the toaster. He started to shave, listening to the eight o'clock news on the radio.

". . . to the teachers' strike. Officials of the GTU are due to meet management tomorrow. A six-year-old boy has been missing from his home in High Wycombe since five o'clock yesterday evening. The police are anxious to trace the boy's father, Perry Barker. When last seen, Mr. Barker was driving a Renault 6, registration number 826 HW 2. A freak accident in a cottage near Wincanton ended in tragedy last night. An explosion believed to be caused by a leakage of gas completely destroyed the cottage, setting the premises on fire. Neighbours alerted the Wincanton Fire Brigade but by the time they arrived the building was gutted. The bodies of two women were taken to Yeovil Hospital but found to be dead on arrival. One woman has been identified as Emma Murchison, the owner of the cottage. The identity of the second victim has not yet been established . . ."

He silenced the set and leaned hard against the wall, his face still covered with shaving-cream. He scraped the razor over his face, dumped the burnt toast in the garbage-pail, and drank the coffee. It was some time before he could bring himself to dial Pelham's number. The phone had been left off the hook again. Raven dressed, heavy with guilt and remorse. Lauterbach was on deck, curry-combing the Great Dane.

"What happened?" he asked, looking up.

Raven felt for the rail. "That girl you met yesterday, Harriet Horne. She's dead."

Lauterbach heaved himself up, pieces of dog-fur clinging to the hair on his chest. He fumbled for his spectacles.

"You've got to be kidding!"

Raven explained what he had heard. "It isn't an accident. This is murder. Those bastards killed her!"

The American's face was shocked. "I can't believe it," he said, shaking his head.

Raven looked at the dog. "Has that animal had her exercise?"

"As much as she'll get," said Lauterbach. "She's just come in season. Why do you ask?"

"I need your help, Hank," Raven said.

The American nodded. "You got it!"

"There's a guy called Mount, a dealer in first editions. His shop is in Cecil Court, that's between Charing Cross Road and Saint Martin's Lane. Mount's First Editions, he calls himself. He's mixed up in this business, Hank. I want you to go there and nose around."

Lauterbach attached a RangeFree leash to the dog's collar. "Nose around for what?"

"Anything," Raven said impatiently. "See if you can find out if he lives on the premises. If not, find out where he *does* live. I can't afford to show my face anywhere near there."

Lauterbach scratched a skinny elbow. "OK. It's none of my business but isn't it time to start doing these things by numbers? I mean, shouldn't you call in the law?"

"And say what?" Raven asked flatly. The fuse on his temper was burning rapidly. "I'm not exactly flavour of the month with them. I've got no proof, Hank. I've got to go with whatever I have. Will you do it or not?"

"I already said that I'll do it. When do you want me to go?"

Raven's watch was in his bedroom. "Now," he said.

Lauterbach picked up his newspaper. "What time is it?"

"Ten to nine," Raven answered.

Lauterbach stared at him. "How do you know that?"

Raven touched the side of his head. "A clock!" he said. "And try to look respectable."

"Respectable!" Lauterbach repeated, outraged. "I call that a cheap shot."

"The beard!" said Raven. "I'll be back in a few minutes."

He walked back to the *Albatross* and made more coffee. At nine o'clock he called the South West Gas Authority. A man in the Public Affairs Office listened sympathetically.

"I understand your concern, Mister Raven," he said. "I agree, this is a terrible tragedy. But all I'm able to tell you at this juncture is that we have an inspector on site. We're expecting a full report some time later today."

Raven's voice sharpened. "Just how sure can you be that it *was* an accident?"

"I don't think I follow," the official replied. "What exactly did you have in mind?"

Raven hesitated. "I'm thinking of . . ." His voice trailed off.

"Two lives have been lost," said the official. "When something like this happens, the Authority has a duty to the public to establish the facts. There is no question of trying to evade responsibility."

"I understand that," said Raven.

"I have your number," the man said. "I'll make a point of calling you personally the moment we have a statement ready."

Raven glanced through the window. Lauterbach had vanished below with the dog. The bell sounded. Pelham's voice crackled in the entryphone. Raven unlocked a drawer in his desk and took out the Spanish .32. He stuffed the gun behind the chair-cushions and pressed the button, releasing the catch on the door at the foot of the steps.

Pelham came through the bead curtains, hands held defensively. He was unshaven, his eyeballs were red, and the grey silk suit looked as though he had slept in it. One of the sleeves was ripped.

"What's the matter?" Raven asked grimly. "All this too much for your delicate conscience?"

Pelham sat down heavily on the couch. "I gave them the number and that's all, I swear it!"

Raven groped for the gun behind the cushions. "Two innocent women are dead because of you. You poison everything you touch. I've never killed a man in cold blood but by God you deserve it!"

Pelham dropped to his knees in a position of supplication.

"I was no part of what happened, I swear it!"

"Get up," Raven said with contempt. He pushed Pelham back on the couch and switched on the answering-machine. Harriet Horne's voice filled the room.

Pelham hung his head, staring at the floor. "I suppose I'm next on the list."

Raven looked at him. "You're beyond the reach of all human decency. Even now, the only person you can think of is yourself."

Pelham moved his head with the readiness of the coward to admit the truth.

Raven dropped the gun in his pocket. It was easy to make good his threat, the way he was feeling.

"Harriet made a statement to my lawyer before she went to

the country about what happened the night you met her. You told her the truth, remember? How you set Helga up? You beat justice once but this is going to be different. This is conspiracy to murder."

Pelham's tongue slid the length of his lips. He had difficulty finding his voice.

"I want to live," he said humbly. "I want to help put things right."

"Put things right!" Raven reiterated. "What sort of slime does your brain crawl in?"

Pelham had passed beyond shame. "I'll do whatever you say," he pleaded.

Raven stood up. "Your days are probably numbered anyway."

The thought stirred Pelham to fresh endeavour. "We could work something out."

Raven came close, looking down into Pelham's bloodshot eyes. "How do you contact these people?"

Pelham gestured uncertainly. "It used to be through Mount. I'd call him and he'd pass on the message. They told me last night not to call him again."

"You keep saying *they,*" said Raven. "What are their names?"

Pelham gulped . . . "One of them is Saladin. I don't know the other man's name, but he's a doctor. I've never seen anyone else. Business was always conducted through intermediaries."

Raven opened a drawer and took out a small tape-recorder and a couple of spare cassettes. He crooked a finger at Pelham and led the way into the kitchen.

"Sit down!" he said, pointing to a chair. He put the tape-recorder and cassettes in front of Pelham. "Do you know how to work this thing?"

Pelham nodded.

Raven prodded the younger man's chest with a finger. "You're going to put the whole story on tape for me. How you first became involved with the Iranians. Who you met, who you saw. I want the locations of places you went to. How you made your deliveries, who paid you. And I want the truth, right from the beginning. And another thing, who really paid for your defence?"

"They did," said Pelham. He picked up the microphone, his eyes straying to the window. The network of ropes overhead offered an easy escape to the Embankment.

"Don't even think about it," said Raven, shaking his head. "You've got nowhere to go."

Pelham tapped the microphone. He was using his damaged hand more and more.

"I don't know," he said doubtfully. "My head's not too clear. I've been up all night."

"You'll do fine," Raven said. "Just think about spending the rest of your life behind bars."

He turned quickly, hearing someone tapping on the sitting-room window. It was Lauterbach. Raven went out on deck.

"What do you think?" the American asked. He was wearing a sixties seersucker suit, roll-collar shirt, and unpolished chukker boots. The dye had been washed from his beard leaving a straggle of brown and grey hairs.

"You look good," said Raven, walking his friend to the door at the end of the gangway. "Find out whatever you can without making it obvious."

"The one thing I never look is obvious," the American said.

Raven opened the door to the steps. "I've got Pelham in there," he said, nodding back.

Lauterbach let out a starling's whistle. "Don't turn your back."

"I need him where I can see him," said Raven. "I thought of sticking him on your boat."

"No chance," Lauterbach said firmly.

"Only for a few hours," urged Raven. "He's got to be in one piece, making sense."

"Screw him," said Lauterbach. "Find somewhere else for him. I wouldn't sleep easy if he'd been aboard."

He lifted a hand and was gone.

Pelham was still in the kitchen, talking into the microphone. Raven plopped on the couch in front of the television set. There was nothing more on the news about the explosion. Pelham came into the room half-an-hour later. He put the tape-recorder and cassettes on the couch beside Raven.

"It's the best I could do," he mumbled.

"Life's a battle," said Raven. "Sit down over there."

He played the two tapes back. Pelham's style was a mixture of boasting and breast-beating. He talked about expensive hotels, of garages in Brussels, Hamburg, and Amsterdam. Payment for the dope-runs had been made by anonymous couriers, his deliveries made in similar fashion. Pelham spoke of feeling trapped, of being completely alone in the world, forced to go on by circumstances. About Helga Heumann he was most self-revealling.

"It just seemed to happen," his voice whined. "Mount had told me that the next run would be from Amsterdam. That meant I had to start looking for somebody suitable. I'd heard about these tea-dances at the Montcalm Hotel so I went. Helga was sitting alone and I chatted her up. She was perfect. She lapped up everything that I told her. She had a valid International Driving Licence and couldn't wait to come to Amsterdam."

Raven suspended the tape. "How long was she with you in Putney?"

Pelham sucked on his cigarette, his eyes shifty. "Ten days, maybe. I had to hang on there. Mount was waiting for the final details, Helga and I just sat around talking."

"About the farmhouse in Tuscany?"

Sunshine was touching Pelham's unshaven face. He moved a few inches.

"It wasn't the way you think. It was Helga who did most of the talking. She wanted to get married, have kids, that sort of thing."

"Suppose things hadn't gone wrong at Dover," asked Raven. "What did you have in mind for her?"

Pelham pushed a hand through his white hair, a look of surprise on his face. "Dump her, of course." He started to grin but thought better of it. "You know how it goes."

"I don't," Raven said. "Tell me!"

Habit was strong and the grin broke through. "It was over, for God's sake. Finished."

"But Helga didn't know it," Raven said pointedly. "How were you going to break the news?"

Pelham thumbed his cigarette into the ashtray. "Tell her to pack her things, I suppose."

Raven leaned forward. "She'd been living with you for ten days and you were in contact with Mount. She might have noticed something strange going on. Something you said or did that she wrote in her diary."

Pelham rolled his eyes at the ceiling. "We're back to the diary! How many times do I have to tell you, I never saw the sodding diary!"

Raven sealed the two cassettes in a large envelope. "But people are getting killed because of it."

Pelham was watching the envelope. "There goes my death-warrant," he said, shaking his head.

"Don't worry about it." Raven addressed the envelope to Patrick O'Callaghan. "People like you live to be a hundred."

The two men walked along the sunlit deck and stopped at the steps. The river washed over the stone.

"Wait here," instructed Raven. "Don't come up until I give you the signal on the horn. Two long, one short."

Raven stood on the pavement, glancing in both directions. He saw nothing out of the ordinary and hurried up Old Church Street. The O'Callaghan car was parked in the patio. Raven pushed the envelope through the letter-box. It was no time for explanations. He moved the Metro out of the cul-de-sac and beeped on the horn. Pelham appeared at the top of the steps.

"One wrong move," said Raven, "and those tapes go to the law."

He drove to the King's Road supermarket and parked at the rear. He came out carrying a paper sack of provisions, toothbrush and razor. For a second he thought that Pelham had taken off. Then he saw the white head halfway down the back of his seat. Pelham looked up anxiously as Raven opened the door.

"Where am I going?" Pelham asked. He was showing signs of increasing tiredness.

"Where you'll be off the street," answered Raven.

Pelham closed his eyes briefly. "Thank God for that. I'm beginning to see things."

Raven swung the car left into Draycott Place and put the nearside wheels up on the pavement. They had stopped in front of a redbrick Edwardian town house that had been converted into furnished rooms for holiday rental. Raven rang a bell and the door opened. He turned left into an office where a woman removed the cigarette from her mouth.

"Can I help you?" she asked. She spoke with the weariness of someone who asks the same question too many times in one day.

Raven took the chair on the opposite side of the desk. "I'd like a single room for a week, maybe two. If you haven't got a single, I'll take a double."

He knew the place well from the old days. People on the run used to hole up here, sinking into anonymity among students and tourists. The company owned three houses side by side. Each had its own street entrance with access to its neighbour through a door on the top floor.

The manageress consulted a chart on the wall. "I can give you a single. £65 a week, £5 a week service charge. You pay a week's rent in advance and two as deposit."

"I'll take it," said Raven. He placed the money on the desk.

The woman gave him an agreement to sign. "Sheets and towels are changed once a week and the room is cleaned on

Wednesdays. You'll find a bathroom and lavatory on all floors. No musical instruments played after midnight."

He signed the agreement in the name George Barber of Christchurch, New Zealand. The manageress gave him a key.

"This opens your room and the front door. You're in number fifty-seven, room sixteen. I'm here until four o'clock, five days a week."

Worn red carpet covered the stairs of the house next door. The room overlooked Draycott Place from the second floor. It was the size of a police-cell, with a bed, chair, and a wardrobe. There was a small electric grill and some dubious-looking kitchen utensils.

Pelham was sitting in the car with his eyes closed.

"Let's go," said Raven, rapping in the glass, "and bring the groceries with you."

Pelham followed him up the stairs. Raven tossed the key on the bed.

"Take a bath and get some sleep," Raven said. "And don't open this door to anyone except me. I'll be back later."

Once on the street, he glanced up at Pelham's window. The curtain had already been drawn. He called Mrs. Winebert from a payphone on Eaton Terrace.

"It's John Raven. Can I come over and see you? I'd appreciate it."

"O my God!" Her tone was devoid of enthusiasm. "Is there really going to be no end to it? We've been pestered for months over this wretched business. That awful man turning up was the last straw."

"You mean Pelham?"

"Who else?" she said bitterly. "He was everything I expected him to be. Smooth and completely horrible."

"What did he want?"

"He wanted to talk about Helga's funeral, would you believe! At least, that's the excuse he gave. I told him, all we know about it is what they said at the German Embassy. Helga's father arranged for her body to be flown back to Düsseldorf."

"If I could see you for just a few minutes," he coaxed. "It's very important to me, Mrs. Winebert."

She hesitated. "My husband's given me strict instructions. We're trying to forget the whole thing."

"Would you prefer me to ask your husband?" he queried.

"I don't advise that," she said quickly. "When were you thinking of coming?"

"Right now," he said. "I can be there in the time it takes to come from Sloane Square."

She agreed reluctantly. "OK, then I'll wait in for you. But I warn you this is definitely the last time, Mister Raven. We're worried about our daughter. Children can sense things, you know."

Raven made it in thirty-five minutes. Mrs. Winebert opened the street door looking good in a white skirt and sleeveless lilac top. Her hair was pinned up. She ushered him into the piano-room, her manner politely reserved.

"Can we get this over quickly?" she asked. "I have shopping to do."

Papers lifted on top of the piano. A breeze blew through the French windows. Raven's smile felt as though it came through five layers of Max Factor Pan-Cake.

"It's the diary," he admitted.

She touched the back of her upswept hair. The movement revealed a shaven armpit.

"Not that again, surely!" she cried. "The poor girl's dead and buried for God's sake. Why can't we leave her in peace?"

"It wouldn't mean leaving her in peace," he maintained. "It would be betraying her. I haven't been idle, Mrs. Winebert. I've learned a lot in the last few days." A frown tugged at her forehead. "I'm still not quite sure what it is that you're meant to be doing."

The sides of his mouth curved up. "There's a solid body of opinion that would agree with you. No matter, what I'm trying to do is prove that Helga was innocent."

She clasped one knee over the other. "Let me be frank with

you, Mister Raven. My husband and I have been sickened and distressed by this whole affair. You spoke about writing a book. What's going to happen when it's published? People are going to start talking again. Don't you see the position this will put us in?"

"I do," he agreed. "But that doesn't alter the fact that an innocent girl was convicted. I've now got definite proof of this, Mrs. Winebert. Surely the truth matters more than personal feelings?"

She glanced sideways at her reflection in the mirror. "That makes me sound totally callous and I'm not. Nor is Roger. I've explained how we felt about Helga. It's just that . . ." She broke off and shook her head.

He tried to get through to her. "Look, if this book ever gets published I can assure you of one thing, your names won't be mentioned."

She was unmoved. "With the best will in the world, Mister Raven, there's nothing more I can do to help you."

A thought became words. "Would you let me take a quick look at Helga's room?"

"Helga's *room?*" Mrs. Winebert was plainly puzzled. "What on earth for? It's been empty since Helga left. We've rather given up on *au-pairs!*"

It was no more than a feeling. Like a face in a crowd, a name remembered.

"I wouldn't be long," he persisted.

She glanced at the clock and smoothed her skirt. "OK," she said.

He followed her up the stairs. She opened a door on the top landing.

"It's just as she left it," she said. "Give me a shout when you've finished. I'll be downstairs."

It was a bright room with Habitat furniture and a flowered duvet and curtains. The window looked down on the garden. There was a small colour TV and a rack full of paperbacks in German. He opened the clothes-closet on a line of empty hangers and moved to the wing-mirror dressingtable. There was a ball of twine in the small drawer on the left, a sheet of folded wrapping paper, and some green sealing-wax in the other drawer.

He called over the banister, displaying his find. "Are these things yours, Mrs. Winebert?"

She climbed a few stairs to see better. "No," she replied. "They must have been Helga's."

He searched the remaining drawers but found nothing. Mrs. Winebert was waiting in the hallway.

"Would you mind if I keep this paper and stuff?" he enquired.

"Of course," she said, waving a hand. "Have you finished upstairs?"

"Completely." He smiled. "I'm very grateful for your patience with me, Mrs. Winebert. I won't be bothering you again. I'll let you know how the book comes out."

Back in the car, he examined his find more closely. The wrapping-paper and twine had been cut with some sharp instrument. The wick on the sealing-wax had been burned. Suddenly he knew the truth. Helga Heumann had wrapped a package up in that room. Instinct told him what it was. She must have done it when she came back to collect her belongings. By then, she'd been living with Pelham for almost a week.

Raven returned to the boat. Lauterbach was lying on deck, his head cradled against the Great Dane's flank. The massive dog lay asleep, its muzzle between its paws, indifferent to the flies that swarmed near the scraps of fishbait. Raven went across.

"OK, what happened?" he asked.

Lauterbach rolled on his side, looking up. "I don't think it's healthy to be seen talking to you."

"You're a fearless fellow," said Raven. "Are you going to tell me what happened or not?"

Lauterbach scrambled up. "Your friend Mount is currently

reposing in the Horseferry Road Mortuary. In a state of rigor mortis as the saying goes."

Heat had softened the pitch in the deck seams. Raven steadied himself against the rail, picking a lump of tar from the sole of his shoe. He kept his voice under control.

"I'm going through a difficult time, Hank."

The American waved a hand. "The store was shut when I got there, boards nailed across the door where the lock had been broken. The guy in the store next door said that the police had done it."

Raven looked at him. "You're really enjoying this, aren't you? Why don't you get to the bloody point?"

Lauterbach pushed up his spectacles. The new-style beard made him older in appearance.

"What an impatient little man you are! Mount had a date with a VAT inspector at half-past nine this morning. The inspector arrived and found the place shut. Nobody answered the phone so after a while he called in the law. They broke down the door. You don't mess with the VAT," he said with the voice of bitter experience.

Lauterbach caught Raven's eye and continued. "The guy who's telling me all this went upstairs with the cops. They found Mount hanging from the chandelier. They had to cut him down, stiff as a poker. It wasn't a pleasant experience by all accounts."

"It rarely is," said Raven. "So you came on home?"

The American stuck his tongue in his cheek. "I walked to the salt-beef bar on the corner and bought myself a pastrami on rye. The guy waiting table told me the whole story. By that time the CID had arrived. They had their breakfast in the salt-beef bar. According to them, Mount was suffering from terminal cancer. A clear case of suicide."

"You're sucking wind," said Raven.

Lauterbach cocked his head. "How do you mean?"

"Let's put it another way. Are you a betting man, Hank?"

"It's been known," Lauterbach said cautiously.

"Then bet your ass on a certainty," Raven said. "That was no suicide. Notice anyone hanging around since you got home?"

The American jerked his thumb at the boy on the mud-flats. "Only him."

"I'll talk to you later," said Raven.

He closed the curtains in his sittingroom. It was Mrs. Burrows' rest-day. The door at the bottom of the steps was locked. Lauterbach was no invader of privacy. Raven opened a drawer in his desk. He had collected a file of newspaper cuttings about the trial. Among these was a picture of Helga Heumann getting out of a police-car flanked by two Drugs Squad officers. AU-PAIR ACCUSED OF HEROIN SMUGGLING. He tore off the caption and pocketed the photograph. Of one thing he was certain. Mrs. Winebert's neighbour had seen the couple arrive. Pelham had stayed outside in the car while Helga went into the house. She'd had ample time to parcel the diary and hide it among her clothes. She must have mailed it some time between then and her arrest. What had she learned about Pelham, why the secrecy?

He was sure now what he had to do. He drove to Beech Avenue, parked outside Pelham's house, and walked up the driveway. He looked through the kitchen windows. Footsteps tracked through the mess on the floor. He could see the hallway, the confusion in the room beyond. An empty cigarette-pack floated on the surface of the pool. He turned quickly, sensing that he was being watched. The windows were blank. He retraced his steps to the Metro, putting himself in Helga's place. Pelham had left her alone in the house on several occasions. What easier than walk to the nearest post office.

He turned the car east towards Putney High Street. There was a post office close to the public library. Raven walked to the end of the counter. A sign read PARCELS.

"I need some advice," Raven said to the clerk. "A friend of mine sent a parcel from here a few weeks ago. It didn't arrive at the destination. She's asked me to make some enquiries."

"You're sure it was sent from here?"

"That's what she says."

The clerk laid a form on the counter. "Tell her to fill this in. The instructions are on the back."

Raven produced the picture of Helga. "This is the lady I'm talking about. Perhaps you remember her face?"

The man's glance was perfunctory. "We get a couple of hundred customers through here every day. By the time five o'clock comes they all look alike."

Raven went out to the car. He lowered the sun-visor and studied the form he had been given. The instructions covered two-thirds of one page.

ENQUIRIES ABOUT A MISSING OR DAMAGED PARCEL COMPLETE THIS SECTION

Name, address and telephone number.

State contents of package, whether name and address of recipient incorrect or insufficient. If so, state what the full name and address should have been.

He tore the form in small pieces. There had to be more than one post office in the neighbourhood. He drove west along Upper Richmond Road, scanning the buildings on both sides. He braked hard suddenly. A sign supplied by a tobacco-company bore the name G. SINGH. Raven could see the interior of the sub-post office through the store window. Display racks carried greeting-cards and stationery. A stout woman with oiled black hair and wearing pantaloons stood at the cigarette-counter.

A bell jangled as Raven opened the door. A heavy grid stretched across the counter at the end of the room. A whiskered, bearded, and turbaned Sikh looked up from behind the grid. Gold-rimmed spectacles enlarged eyes like chestnuts swimming in glycerine.

Raven bought a packet of Gitanes from the woman and turned to the man. "Mister Singh?"

The Sikh inspected as much of Raven as he could see through the grid. Two time-locked safes were set in the wall behind him.

"Sorry, sir. Post office closed for lunch."

He moved a little nearer the panic-button that rang an alarm in the local police-station.

Raven pulled his warrant-card from his pocket, his thumb concealing the obsolete date of issue. There was no one else in the shop.

The Sikh's manner was agitated. "Why you are coming here, Officer?"

Raven leaned against the counter. "This isn't an official visit," he said reassuringly. "I'm just making a few enquiries. Do you remember this lady?"

The Sikh looked at Helga's picture and shook his head. There was a strong smell of curry about him.

"Who is this person, please?"

Raven returned the warrant-card to his pocket. "You must remember her, surely, Mister Singh. She was staying on Beech Avenue. German, about so tall." He marked her height with a hand.

The Sikh's eyes sought his wife's help. "We have people here all the time, Officer. We are paying out pensions and family allowances. Many post office matters." His confidence grew with the thought.

"How about you, Mrs. Singh?" Raven asked, showing her Helga's picture.

Her husband broke in quickly. "We are honest people obeying all laws. We have been here ten years from Uganda and not one single complaint!"

Raven smiled. "Let's get this straight, Mister Singh. This isn't a complaint. I'm asking for help."

The woman waddled from the counter and inspected the photograph. She showed a set of perfect teeth to her husband.

"You remember, Gobind! So nice, so pleasant young girl. Not like some who come here. Respectful!"

The Sikh's face was grave. "We have seen her again on television. Such a shock! Very, very sad. Sometimes she spoke to my wife about Germany. We have relatives living in Frankfurt."

"She brought in a parcel," said Raven. "Do you remember that? It was some time in April."

One memory stirred another. "A *registered* parcel," the Sikh amended. "The string was not tied according to regulations. She had to do over again. Yes, a *registered* parcel."

Hope flooded Raven's brain. "Where was the parcel sent to?"

The Sikh muttered something and placed a thick book on the counter between them. Singh found the appropriate page, a ringed hand holding the book tight. A duplicate counterfoil gave the information.

NAME OF SENDER
Helga Heumann 48 Beech Avenue Putney SW 16
NAME OF ADDRESSEE
Wolf Heumann Haus Sägerwerk Bei Rath Düsseldorf

The date of dispatch was April 12, a week after Helga met Pelham. A look of worry spread across the Sikh's face. "The parcel has not been received?" he asked anxiously.

"No problem," said Raven. "I needed to know the date it was sent. Thanks for your help."

Back on the boat, he obtained the number from International Directory Enquiries. A man's voice answered Raven's call.

"Heumann!"

Raven put the phone down quickly and re-dialled. O'Callaghan's secretary answered.

"It's me, Anne," said Raven. "Is he there?"

"I'll put you through," she replied.

"Can you meet me at six o'clock?" asked Raven. "It's important that we meet—Ocho Rios, OK?"

"I suppose so," the lawyer said grudgingly. "But it won't be for long. We're out for supper."

The Ocho Rios was a bar on Park Walk, a hangout for out-of-work actors and actresses. It was a place where reggae music was played and few listened. A loose-limbed Barbadian took

Raven's order. O'Callaghan came in minutes later, pinstriped, his bow-tie askew as usual. He dropped his briefcase on the floor and tasted the margarita that was waiting for him.

"Women clients!" he complained. "I've got this crank who calls me at all times of the day and night, wanting to change her will. She's done it nine times in the past eighteen months. The joke is, of course, she's got nothing to leave but debts."

"Did you listen to your radio this morning?" asked Raven.

The lawyer finished the rest of his drink and called for two more. "I don't have time to listen."

"Too bad," said Raven. "Harriet Horne's dead."

"Harriet Horne," the lawyer repeated. His face cleared. "You mean Pelham's girlfriend. What happened?"

"Have you come straight from the office?" said Raven. The refills were on the table. "Yes, I have," said the lawyer.

Raven leaned across, dropping his voice. "I dropped a couple of tapes through your letter-box earlier. Pelham made a confession this morning. He got drunk the night he met Harriet and told her the truth about how he set up Helga. That's what's on the tapes."

"You said Harriet was dead."

"She is," said Raven. "She called me at one o'clock in the morning to say that Pelham's house had been burgled. She said she was in desperate trouble, that Pelham had pissed off. In the end I went over to get her. She spent the night on the boat. That's when she told me about Pelham getting drunk. I thought her life was in danger, Patrick. So I drove her down to Somerset to stay with a schoolfriend. I didn't get home until after midnight. She'd left a message on my answering-machine, asking me to call her back immediately. When I did call there was no answer. Do you want me to tell you why?"

"I can guess," said the lawyer. "She was dead."

"They were both dead," said Raven. "She and her friend. Blown into small pieces. The gas people say it was an accident. I say it was murder."

O'Callaghan lit a Turkish cigarette, holding it between thumb and forefinger like a pen. He exhaled in small puffs.

"Do you know who I mean by Mount?" Raven asked.

O'Callaghan's eyes were alert. "The bookdealer?"

"Pelham's contact with the Iranians. I sent Hank Lauterbach over to Mount's shop this morning. The place was closed. The police found Mount hanging from a chandelier. You're not going to tell me that's a coincidence. *We're dealing with killers!* Pelham's the next on the list, of course. I want you to put those tapes in your safe."

"That means you've got Pelham hidden away somewhere."

Raven nodded. "It isn't necessary for you to know where."

The lawyer blocked the suggestion with uplifted hand. "I don't even *want* to know. He isn't my problem, you are."

"I'd be happy to see the bastard dead," said Raven. "But I need him, Patrick."

The lawyer stared hard at him. "Need him for *what?*"

"Pelham's the bait. As long as these people don't know where he is they'll keep looking for him."

"Won't they be looking for you as well?" O'Callaghan's eyes were half-closed.

Raven shrugged. "It's a fair assumption. But I'm an entirely different proposition!"

"And modest with it," the lawyer replied.

Raven flicked his cigarette at the ashtray. "The diary's what matters. They think I know where it is."

The lawyer's look was curious. *"Do* you?"

"I'm getting close," Raven said.

The lawyer moved his head from side to side. "I wish we didn't have to do this so often, John. I find it a total waste of time."

Raven put his glass down and wiped the salt from his lips. "Why not admit it, it jars your mind when I'm right."

"It worries me even more than usual," the lawyer admitted.

"But *why?*" Raven insisted. The noise of the music was deafening. "I've already got Pelham's confession. With the diary we'll have enough to put these people away for life."

"You keep saying *we,*" the lawyer objected.

"OK, me," said Raven.

"Do you know what you've done?" asked his friend. "You've created a lawyer's nightmare. Facts without proof! You can't even prove that these Iranians exist, for crissakes!"

"Pelham can," Raven retorted.

O'Callaghan's face was closed. "Testimony of a fellow conspirator."

"I know about murder," said Raven. "You keep those tapes in your safe. "I'll do the rest."

"Do you still keep my card in your wallet?" asked the lawyer.

Raven tapped his pocket. "Right here with my blood-type."

"Let's hope you don't have to use either of them," O'Callaghan answered. "When does Kirstie get back?"

Raven drew a deep breath. "Why is it you always change the subject when you run out of argument?"

"I was hoping that she'd be able to talk some sense into you."

Raven placed both elbows on the table. "What you'd like me to do is drop the whole thing, right?"

"I'd like you to use your head," said his friend. "You don't seem to realise what a pain in the ass you are to the police, John. I mean I've heard them say so, some of them are men of goodwill. Of all people you should know this. They like dealing with things in their own way, saluting one another, getting the computer charts out and so forth. OK, a few villains escape the net but the fabric of law and order is seen to be whole. And that's how they like it. Continue to plague them and they'll fix your wagon for keeps. And that *would* worry me."

"I've got right on my side," Raven argued.

"See how much help it is when you're cracking rocks in the quarry," the lawyer replied. "And don't think I'm kidding. I talk to these people. It's part of my job to talk to these people.

They're content to bide their time. But one of these days they'll get you." He turned down his thumb.

Raven signalled the waiter for the bill. "Then I'll have to be careful, won't I? In the meantime I need the name and address of a lawyer in Düsseldorf."

"Düsseldorf?" O'Callaghan straightened his bowler. "What sort of lawyer?"

"A criminal lawyer," said Raven. "Someone who speaks good English. Someone like you."

"Why would you need a lawyer in Düsseldorf?"

"I may need someone to hold my hand. That's where I'm going."

"And what about Kirstie?"

"You take care of Maureen and I'll take care of Kirstie," said Raven. "Just get me the name of a lawyer."

"I'll have to think," said his friend. "When are you going?"

"Soon," Raven said vaguely.

They made their way outside through the babble and Raven unlocked the Metro. The lawyer mopped his neck with his handkerchief.

"That bloody drink always makes me sweat. Does this mean that you trust Pelham?"

"Not one inch," answered Raven, buckling his seatbelt. "The only thing that's keeping him pointed in the right direction is a healthy respect for his life. I'm going to keep that respect alive. Fasten your belt."

The lawyer obeyed. "I always thought you spoke German."

"I did," said Raven. He let in the clutch and the car moved forward. "But that was thirty years ago. I wouldn't be sure of it in the cut-and-thrust of a German police-station."

The lawyer made a sound of despair. "We're in the police-station now, are we?"

Raven swung left onto Church Street. "When I'm sure I try not to be certain."

He stopped outside the lawyer's house. "Give my love to Maureen."

He left the car in the alleyway and went down the steps. Daylight was fading fast. The tide had turned, lifting the boats. A few lights twinkled on the neighbouring craft. More lights burned in the pub and the parking-lot opposite. It was quiet on his boat, away from the noise of the traffic. The air had the salt reek of tidal water. The one thing missing was Kirstie. Home wasn't home without her. He walked along the deck a few yards and stopped dead. For the second time that day he felt he was being watched. He moved into the shadow at the end of the deck and glanced along the stone parapet overhead. It was empty. He unlocked the door to his sittingroom. He was met by the familiar smell of roses and furniture-polish. The first message on the answering-machine was from the South West Gas Authority.

"This is Paul Harrap, Mister Raven. I promised I'd call you back. I've got a copy of the Inspector's report in front of me. I won't bother you with the technical details but this is the thrust of the matter. The explosion in Miss Murchison's cottage was due to a buildup of gas originating somewhere in the kitchen. The extent of the damage makes it virtually impossible to determine the exact source of the leak but spontaneous combustion is out of the question. The triggering device must have been a spark or a naked flame. If you want any further information, I suggest you get in touch with the Wincanton police. Ask for Superintendent Bailey."

The tape continued. Raven heard the sound of a coin dropping in a payphone meter then the buzz of an empty line. He tried again. First came the dialling tone, the drop of a coin making connection, then silence. Not even the sound of breathing.

He took his fieldglasses out on deck and climbed on top of the superstructure. He had a clear view of the front of the pub and the parking-lot. There had been three cars when last he looked. Now there were four. The new arrival was drawn up under the trees. A man emerged from the pub as Raven watched. Raven focused, dragging the man within touching distance. He wore a light tan suit, dark glasses and no hat. He unlocked the car near the trees and sat behind the wheel, his head turned in the direction of the *Albatross.*

Raven jumped down hastily and hurried inside. He switched off the lights and sat in the dimness. His telephone number had been unlisted since he had left the police-force. He sat for half-an-hour waiting for the next move to be made. Nothing happened. When he went out on deck again the fourth car had gone. He had taken the registration numbers but with Jerry Soo in Hong Kong, ownership would be hard to trace. He knew in the bedrock of his brain that the man he had seen was an Iranian. Ingersoll Harry's parting gift to Raven was hidden down in the hold. Raven shifted the refrigerator and lifted the hatch in the floor. The suede jewellery-roll was concealed among the winebottles. Ingersoll Harry had broken his back in a fall from an eighteenth floor window. The deathbed interview had been conducted with style and humour. Both were supplied by the burglar. Raven was an honourary thief, he said. And he should have the tools of the trade. The collection of skeleton and master keys were handmade from surgical steel. So were the probes and lockpicks.

Raven tore the labels from a shirt and from one of his windbreakers. He stuffed the clothing into a plastic bag. He left the sittingroom light burning and the doors to the deck locked. He scrambled over the end rail and worked his way from boat to boat. A chorus of barking dogs followed. The next flight of steps were identical with his own. The lamp at the top had long since been vandalised. He climbed up cautiously, looking right and left when he reached the top. He was certain now that his car would be watched. He crossed the Embankment and walked up Old Church Street. Lights showed in the O'Callaghan house but their car was missing. Raven kept on walking towards King's Road. For the last twenty years he had always known when he was being followed. There was nobody on his tail at the moment.

He stopped a taxi that took him to Queen's Gate and walked

through to the mews. Victorian lamp-posts lit the short length of cobble-stones. The door to Pelham's flat was flush with the wall and afforded no cover. He stood with his back to the group of people drinking outside the pub and inspected the cheap Yale-type lock. The first master-key he used turned it off. He stepped inside, pulling the door shut and stood in the tiny hallway, his eyes adjusting to the darkness. A flight of stairs led to the upper floor. There was another door at the top. He climbed the stairs splay-legged, distributing his weight on the outside of each tread in case of a creaking board. He ran his fingers over the door's painted surface, finding the outline of a mortice lock. The third key he tried lifted the levers. Enough light came from the mews for Raven to make out the bed and furniture. A canvas bag on a chair carried a KLM label. Inside was a change of clothing. Pelham's story was holding up, Raven moved to the window. Nothing had changed in the mews. He let himself out of the flat and walked towards Queen's Gate at an even pace, looking straight ahead.

He had no illusions about the people he was up against. They were a different breed to the thieves he had known, spurred by fanaticism instead of greed. There was no doubt in Raven's mind that they would kill again to achieve their objective. The crescent moon carried an aureole and it was much cooler. He strolled along Draycott Place, looking up at Pelham's window. A light showed through a gap in the curtains. He used his keys on the door to the house next door and stepped into the silent hallway. A smell of cooking permeated the landings. He crossed from the top of one house to the other and tapped softly on Pelham's door.

"Open up, it's me!"

He heard the bedspring groan then Pelham appeared, wrapped in a bath-towel. He had shaved and looked rested.

"Mount's dead," said Raven.

Pelham flushed to the roots of his white hair. "Jesus *Christ!*"

"He was hanged," Raven said bleakly.

Pelham sank down on the bed, looking up. "I can't stand any more of this," he said brokenly. "You said I'd be safe."

"Do as you're told and you will be." Raven threw the plastic bag on the bed beside Pelham. "We're leaving the country."

Pelham lit a cigarette, his cupped hands trembling. "They've got my passport."

Raven closed the gap in the curtains. "We'll get you something else in the morning. You'll need a copy of your birth certificate. There are some things you can wear in the bag."

Pelham's colour was back to normal. "Where are we going?"

"You ask too many questions," Raven answered.

Pelham blew smoke at the floor, shaking his head. "I'm finished in this country anyway."

"Good thinking," said Raven. "I'll be here at nine o'clock sharp in the morning. I want you dressed and ready to go. In the meantime the same rules apply. Keep the door locked and don't leave the house."

"Whatever you say." Pelham was very subdued.

Raven let himself out to Draycott Place. The first drops of rain spattered the pavement. A bus took him to the top of Beaufort Street. It was another ten minutes to the *Albatross.* A glow showed in Lauterbach's portholes but Raven was in no mood for talk. He put the burglar tools back in their hiding-place and shut the curtains. Familiar noises outside heightened the quiet on the boat. He cut all the lights except the one over his Klee. The rest of the long room lay in shadow. He poured himself a scotch and stretched out on the couch. He pulled up his jeans on impulse and inspected the calves of both legs. His skin was smooth where the varicose veins had been excised. He was as fit as he'd been in years.

The scotch found its way to his brain, floating a memory that had long been submerged. The note on his desk in the Serious Crimes Squad Room had summoned him to the Assistant Commissioner's office. He remembered the way the other people in the room had found things to do as he walked to the door. No one had looked at him. He'd been expecting the summons for days. He remembered the Assistant Commissioner's room, the photographs of Assistant Commissioner Soames at an Interpol convention, receiving the OBE. Above all, he remembered the face of the man at the desk, the aura of high moral rectitude.

Soames' expression had been tinged with regret as he opened then closed Raven's file.

"There's not really much to be said, Detective-Inspector. You were offered a Board of Enquiry and refused it."

It was weird the way they had narrowed things down, a Board of Enquiry or suspension on half-pay. All this for exposing a crooked cop, a scumbag who'd been on the take for twelve years.

Soames seized upon Raven's silence. "You're a highly intelligent man with a record that looks fine on paper. But you have one basic problem, Detective-Inspector. You think you can make your own rules. This force is based on loyalty, a chain of command. No officer is expected to exceed the duties and responsibilities delegated to him. There's no place for a man who takes the law into his own hands."

"Drake was tried in a court of law," Raven said. "A jury found him guilty."

"You're finished," said Soames.

Raven remembered his slow walk to the door, his grin as he lived that last moment.

"You're right about one thing, Assistant-Commissioner. There's no place for me on the force. You can stuff the pension and anything else I have coming. I need a change of scenery. I quit!"

He took his empty glass into the kitchen. As Patrick O'Callaghan said, nothing has changed. He was still making his own rules and would continue to do it as long as he could. He scrambled some eggs with an ounce of caviare and ate from the pan standing up. He dropped the pan in the sink and undressed, aiming his clothes in the direction of the bathroom. They were playing *The Thomas Crown Affair* on Channel 2. He watched it from the bed, seeing it for the third time, his head haunted by the theme-song.

Kirstie stared at him from the silver frame on the dressing-table. He tried to see himself as she saw him and failed. The late news finished and the weather announcer took over with a touch of humour as he talked about satellite pictures and deep depressions. He had good news for farmers and ducks, he said. It would rain tonight and tomorrow and for the next few days.

Raven extinguished the light and slept.

CHAPTER 7

Pelham woke to the sound of the man in the room next door, hawking and spitting. Traffic lumbered past the rainwashed windows. It took an effort to pull himself together, to put people and places in proper perspective. He propped on an elbow and looked at his watch. It was twenty minutes to eight, a little more than an hour before Raven arrived. Pelham had his own idea about the ex-cop. Nobody spent that length of time on the CID without being touched with larceny.

He got out of bed and opened a crack in the door. The bathroom was free. He grabbed his towel, a razor, and toothbrush and hurried across the landing. He lay in the tub, thinking about where Raven was taking him. The prospect of leaving England eased Pelham's anxiety. He had plans of his own, no matter what Raven was thinking. Survival was the name of the game. He towelled himself dry and made sure that the landing was clear before going back to his room.

His trousers had been on the heat-register overnight, his jacket was rumpled and stained. He pulled on the trousers and donned the shirt Raven had left. The label had been removed from the windbreaker. He looked at himself in the mirror. He was ten years younger than yesterday. He fixed some tea and a bacon sandwich and sat on a chair by the window. Rain fell on glistening pavements, bounced off the upturned umbrellas as pedestrians hurried towards the Sloane Square Underground Station. He counted the cash in his pockets, watching the slow-moving line of traffic. The Iranians had left him with a little more than eight pounds, the price of a round of drinks. They'd taken his checkbook and credit cards. There was no way of getting at the few hundred pounds that remained in the bank. Lack of money was another reason for staying close to Raven. He needed money to run if things should go sour on him. A car horn sounded below. A black Renault had stopped close to the kerb. Pelham ran down the stairs. Raven was at the wheel of the Renault. An umbrella lay on the rear seat.

"Get in," said Raven.

Sixteen hours' rain had turned the city into a nightmare of muddy streets and short tempers. Traffic inched forward, fender to fender, spraying slush over hapless pedestrians. It was the first time Pelham had seen Raven wearing a suit, a grey check with a pale blue shirt and black tasseled loafers. His hair was neatly arranged to cover his ears. Raven turned the Renault south onto Lower Sloane Street. He stamped on the accelerator, beating a bus to the signals at Royal Hospital Road.

Raven peered through swishing windshield wipers. "No problems back there?"

"No problems," said Pelham. "I haven't seen a soul except you since I've been in the place."

An Avis tag hung from the ignition keys. Raven took the river route along the Embankment as far as Blackfriars Bridge. Signals held them again.

"You know what to ask for," said Raven. "A short copy of your birth certificate. It shouldn't take long at this time of day."

The lights started to change. Someone pounded a horn behind. Raven waited for the green before moving.

"Why did you ask where Helga was buried?"

Pelham kept his eyes straight ahead. "I'd have thought that was obvious."

Raven glanced briefly sideways. "There's only one thing obvious about you. What's in it for Pelham."

"No feelings at all, is that it?" asked Pelham.

Raven smiled. "How much money have you got?"

Pelham made a show of slapping his pockets. "About eight quid."

"There's a tenner in the glove-compartment. Take it," said Raven. He drew up outside a grey stone building at the bottom of Kingsway. "I'll hang on here as long as I can. If I'm not here when you come out, wait in the entrance."

Pelham entered the building. A central aisle split the long hall in two. The shelves on each side were crammed with hundreds of leatherbound volumes displayed in alphabetical and chronological order. He carried one to a stand and copied the details on a form. He was out in under fifteen minutes. The Renault was parked in the same place. Pelham climbed in and put the document on Raven's lap.

NAME AND SURNAME		Piers Pelham
SEX		Boy
PLACE	REGISTRATION	
OF	DISTRICT	Newbury
BIRTH	SUB-DISTRICT	Newbury

Certified to have been copied from records in the custody of the Registrar-General given at the Central Register Office under the seal of the said office this 30th day of September.

Raven returned the birth certificate. "Now you need pictures."

He turned left into Covent Garden and filtered through narrow streets to the bottom of Charing Cross Road. He nodded at the steps going down to the Underground station.

"There's a machine in the booking-hall. I'll hang on here."

Coin-operated lights flashed as Pelham sat on a stool behind curtains. He waited five minutes for the prints to be developed and walked back to the car.

Raven took a look at the four photographs, pocketed two and gave the remaining pair to Pelham.

Raven pointed at the post office opposite. "If they ask you if you've already got a passport you say no, OK?"

"I'll need more money," said Pelham.

Raven gave him another ten.

It was one of the larger post offices selling first-issue stamps and commemorative coins. There was no one at the counter dealing with travel-documents. Pelham put the birth certificate and photographs on the counter. A clerk appeared behind the grid. He pushed a form in Pelham's direction. Pelham completed it.

"I'll need something to support this address that you've given," the clerk said.

The demand took Pelham completely by surprise. His pockets were empty except for the money and the key to Draycott Place.

"I don't understand," he replied. "That's where I live, Beech Avenue SW 16."

"That may well be so," said the clerk. "But I still need some verification. You must have something with your address on it. A health-card or driving license. A letter will do."

"Do you see what it's like out there?" Pelham asked, pointing at the rain-sodden street. "I just got soaked. I had to change my jacket in the lavatory in Victoria Station. My wife's there waiting for me. We've got a boat-train to catch."

The clerk retained a tight hold on the pictures and birth certificate. "Where's your ticket?"

"With the rest of my things. My wife's got them."

Unexpected aid came from a middle-aged woman behind. "They're not so fussy when it comes to paying their bills," she sniffed. "As long as it's money, they'll take it, no questions asked!"

The clerk bent to get a better view through the grid. "Suppose you let me take care of this, madam."

"Look in the phone-book!" urged Pelham.

The clerk reached for the directory, glanced at a page, and closed the covers. He turned his back and fixed one of Pelham's photographs to a white cardboard document.

"That'll be seven pounds fifty," he said. "Valid for one year, holidays and unpaid business-trips only."

The clerk switched his displeasure to the woman waiting.

"Things would be a lot easier round here if some people minded their own business."

Pelham left rapidly. It was difficult to tell what was in Raven's mind as he looked at the travel-document.

"We have to talk," he said finally.

He drove back to Chelsea and parked on Limerston Street. They walked side by side under the umbrella to the cafe at the end of the street. Raven ordered coffee and pulled out a Lufthansa folder. He passed it across the table.

"Flight 051 to Düsseldorf. Terminal Two, Heathrow, nine-fifteen tomorrow morning. You get there at eight.

Pelham opened the folder, his pulse beating faster. There was a card clipped to the flight-ticket. HOTEL AM ZOO. A note for a hundred D-marks was folded inside the ticket.

"Take a cab from the airport," Raven instructed. "Your room's booked at the Hotel am Zoo. When you get there just sit and wait. I'll contact you later."

Pelham put the folder in his inside pocket. "OK, you say I ask too many questions, but don't I have a right to know what happens once we get there?"

Raven peered through the cigarette-smoke, his eyes half-closed. "If there's a medal awarded for being a tapeworm, I'll see that you get it."

"You don't give up, do you," Pelham said resentfully. "Aren't you ever going to stop pointing the finger at me? I thought we'd got some sort of relationship going."

"We have," said Raven. "Stay alive for the next couple of days and I'll let you run. And I'll give you a thousand pounds to run with."

"The light at the end of the tunnel." Pelham's tone was sarcastic.

"Don't count on that," said Raven. "It could be a train travelling in the opposite direction."

The man was actually smiling, thought Pelham. His next words were delivered with feeling.

"Could I ask you one favor. I'd like to see my mother before I go."

"Your *mother!*" Raven's eyes were curious. "What brings this on? You've been a shit to your mother since the day you were born."

"Perhaps that's the reason," said Pelham. "The way things are going I may never see her again."

"How long is it since you've seen her?" asked Raven.

"March," said Pelham. "She's a worrier." That much was true.

"Where does she live?"

Pelham gestured towards the river. "Palmerston Mansions. It's just round the corner."

"I know where it is," Raven answered. "She's crippled, isn't she?"

"There's a home-help who comes in every day," said Pelham. "And the neighbours keep an eye on her."

"What would she think if you turned up with me?"

Pelham widened his arms. "I'd have to think of something. Say that you're someone I'm doing some business with. I don't know."

Raven put coins on the table and picked up his umbrella. "Let's move it."

They crossed King's Road to a florist. A girl in a green smock came forward.

"I'd like a dozen red roses," said Raven. "And be sure that you make them look as pretty as you are."

She wrapped the bouquet in see-through cellophane with a ribbon tied round the stems. He gave her the money.

"Almost as pretty!" he said. "Thank you."

Raven stood outside with the flowers, the rain dripping from the umbrella.

"Suppose I were to let you go by yourself, what happens?"

"I'd be more in your debt than ever," said Pelham.

"I don't like emotional scenes," Raven answered. "I don't even know why I'm doing this. You're still going to screw me the moment you can. But nothing's more certain than this. If you're not on that plane in the morning, you'll be committing suicide."

"I know that," Pelham said humbly.

Raven thrust the roses at him. "Try to make peace with your mother. Stay with her until it's dark and take a cab straight back to Draycott Place. I'll look in on you later."

He turned abruptly and jaywalked through the traffic to the opposite side of the road. Pelham watched from a doorway until he saw the Renault drive off towards the Embankment. The gloomy entrance to Palmerston Mansions showed grave signs of neglect. The porter had died seven years ago and had not been replaced. Property-dealers moved in and out, skimming off whatever profit remained. The smell of fried fish reeked through the badly-lit lobby. Pelham placed his ear against the door to his mother's apartment. A Hoover droned on the far side. The home-help was there. He tiptoed back to the street and used the back way into Saint Stephen's Hospital, mingling with patients and visitors until he exited onto Fulham Road. Again he stood in a doorway, looking for danger. He saw none. There was no mystery why they were going to Düsseldorf. Raven must have located the diary. Somehow he needed Pelham in order to get it. The understanding did nothing to ease Pelham's anxiety. This stuff about writing a book was a cover, Raven was looking for glory. He saw himself as some sort of gangbuster and Pelham could guess the scenario. There'd be a crowded courtroom with the Iranians in the dock, Piers Pelham giving evidence against them. He'd leave the building with a target hanging between his shoulder-blades.

He peeked up the street again. It was almost noon. Francesca should be there by now. He'd give her a few more minutes to settle down. His thoughts skipped to the central problem. Suppose *he* was the one to produce the diary! Not necessarily *find* but produce! That would turn the game around entirely. The Iranians would have to deal with him and for a lot more than a lousy grand. All he had to figure out was a safe way to negotiate. In the meantime he had to keep Raven cool and get hold of some front money. It took money to move independently.

Pelham stepped into a nearby payphone. His mother answered, her voice cracked with anxiety. Pelham pictured the dark rooms stuffed with the possessions she had squirrelled away over the years. Georgian silver and porcelain, worth thousands of pounds. She wouldn't part with a single piece of it.

"It's me, Piers," he replied. "Has anyone called for me?"

"No, dear," she said. "Where have you been? I've been telephoning you for three days."

"I'm staying with friends." Even at that distance she could give him a feeling of claustrophobia.

Her voice sharpened. "You're not in some sort of trouble again, are you?"

"No, I am not in trouble. I never *was* in trouble, Mother. Can't you get that in your head? Look, I don't have time to go into details but I'm doing some business. It's important that if anyone telephones for me that you say that I'm there. Will you do that, Mother?"

She sighed. "O dear, I do wish these things didn't always sound so mysterious."

"Don't be so stupid," he said impatiently. "Don't you trust me or what?"

"Of course I trust you," she said.

"Then why don't you do as I ask? If a man calls and wants to speak to me, say that I've just gone out for something. Or to one of the neighbours."

"It really is too bad the way you treat me, you know," she complained.

"All that is going to change," he promised. "I'm going to Germany for a couple of days on business. And listen . . ."

She sighed. "I'm listening—"

"You can get my room ready. I'll be staying."

"Will you telephone again before you leave?"

"I'll call you from Germany," he said. "Goodbye, Mother!"

He stepped from the booth and walked east along Fulham Road. Lights burned in the second-floor windows. Pelham rang the buzzer and was admitted. He rearranged his collar in the mirror and climbed the stairs, carrying the bouquet of roses. A woman was sitting behind the bar filing her nails. She was a negress of uncertain age with chinese eyes and skin the colour of champagne. Her voice seemed to come from behind her knees.

"Well, for God's sweet sake, look who's here!"

He kissed her and tendered the flowers. "Not a word," she said, holding up a hand. "Not a word until I put these in water!"

Pelham hooked his heels over the rungs of a bar-stool. A red, yellow, and green parakeet eyed him malevolently from its perch a few feet away. The long bar was hung with pictures of cats. Siamese cats and Abyssinian cats, alley-cats, cats with angora fur. A barrelhouse upright piano stood at the far end of the room. The negress returned with the roses in a vase and placed them on a ledge away from the heating-register.

"They're gorgeous! Do you know, you're the first person this year to give me roses? What are you drinking, sugarplum?"

He shook his head. "I don't feel like drinking, Francesca. OK, then, an orange-juice."

It was an hour before the bar would be opened. The room was quiet except for the occasional squawk from the parakeet. He stared into his glass until he had her attention.

"Why are all these things happening to me, Francesca?"

"Good times come, good times go," she said, smiling.

Francesca Frascati had made it the hard way. Daughter of a Trinidadian hooker and a Chinese barber, she had clawed her way up from the gutter. At the age of eighteen she was playing ragtime in a club on Via Veneto. A year later she married a magistrate's son who was a law-student by day, a terrorist by night. Six months after the marriage, he was shot dead in a bank-raid. His widow moved on to London and opened a club for people she liked and people with money. She still played boogie when the mood took her and guarded her secrets closely. Some said she was lesbian.

She dribbled a handful of salted peanuts onto the bar in front of Pelham.

"If it's Harriet you're grieving for, forget it. I knew her a whole lot better than you did. You'd have been pulling one another's wings off if you'd stayed together. It's sad, Piers and it's tragic, but you've got to get it out of your system. What did you do to your hand?"

Much of the pain had gone, but the memory rankled. "An accident."

She sliced lemon into her gin-and-tonic. "Apart from all that, how's life been treating you?"

"Since you ask, I'm completely buggered," he said.

She swept her nail-filings into an ashtray. "Could I get an explanation of that statement?"

He turned the corners of his mouth down. "That's easy enough. The trial cost me every penny I had and I haven't done a deal since. You know what people think; where there's smoke, then there's fire."

"That's what they say," she agreed.

He leaned sideways, looking at her from a different angle. "Are you someone who answers letters, Francesca?"

"That depends on who they're from. What makes you ask?"

He unhooked his heels from the rung on the stool. "I'll probably be behind bars this time next week."

"You're joking, of course!"

"I was never more certain. The American Express. They've been chasing me ever since my arrest. They got a judgement order against me three days ago. The next step's a bankruptcy order."

He walked to the window and stared out at the rain. He turned with a grin on his face.

"That's about all there is to it, I suppose."

She put her lipstick and compact on the shelf behind her, studying him in the mirror.

"I always thought you came from a family with money."

His grin belonged to a mischievous schoolboy. "I've been working on that impression ever since I left Eton. The truth is my father was a librarian in the House of Lords. When he died, his life-insurance just about paid off the mortgage on the flat. My mother still lives there if you want to call it living. She's in a wheelchair."

"How much do you owe?" she asked.

He had a feeling that she was teetering. "Too much, my darling. It's always too much."

She opened her handbag and scribbled a check. "Two hundred," she said. "It's the best I can do. If it will help, take it!"

His voice wavered. "I honestly don't know what to say, Francesca. You're the only person who's listened and helped. I won't forget."

"You will," she said with complete assurance. "You're a handsome rogue and I always had a soft spot for you. I've already written it off as the most expensive bunch of flowers I ever bought. Now I suppose you want to get the check cashed?"

He slid from the stool. "I should have married you and that's the truth!"

"I couldn't afford you." She blew him a kiss as he went through the door.

He let himself out to the street, controlling the impulse to run. He crossed to the bus-stop and stood where she would see him if she looked from the window. The bank was at South Kensington. The cashier turned the check over.

"If you'll sign on the back, Mister Pelham. How do you want the money?"

"Four fifties," he said. It was easier to hide.

The notes were new and in sequence. He tucked them in his shirt pocket and left the bank with a sense of triumph. Things were going his way. Those bastards may have been running him ragged but he still hadn't lost his touch. He let himself into his room and hid the money, passport, and flight-ticket in the refrigerator. Then he took off his clothes and got into bed. If Raven came visiting now, so much the better. But tonight was a time for mild celebration.

CHAPTER 8

The Alitalia flight from Rome had landed. Saladin stationed himself at the rails. It would take some time for the incoming passengers to clear immigration and customs. It was ten-thirty in the morning and the Arrival Hall was crowded with people meeting friends. West Africans came through dressed in flamboyant costumes, Indian women in multicoloured saris, Europeans bronzed by the sun, wind, and sea. Hotel employees holding up boards clustered near the exit.

Saladin leaned out a little farther. Like Saladin himself, Hossein was one of the new breed, a product of the Kotal College and a protégé of the Council of Experts. His appearance in England was a sign of trouble. Trolleys were coming through with baggage bearing Alitalia stickers. Hossein was in the vanguard of the next group of passengers, a small man with a boxy French suit and a light coat that he wore like a cloak around his shoulders. He walked with neat purpose, blackhaired with a thin mouth under a jutting nose. Saladin hurried to meet him.

His offer to take the other man's bag was refused. They walked outside to the waiting car. Saladin took the wheel. Hossein settled back next to him. The windshield-wipers clicked to and fro, clearing the rain. The downpour belonged to April rather than late September. Hossein took a cigarette from a package. It was longer than most, half-paper, half-tobacco. He closed his eyes against the rising smoke.

"The Council is disappointed. There should be no need for my presence. This business has been badly handled."

He flinched as a Jaguar barrelled past, spraying slush on the offside window. Saladin changed lanes.

"I asked for no assistance." The memory of his last meeting with Hossein still rankled.

"It is the Council's wish that I am here." Hossein glanced away, viewing the sodden fields enigmatically.

It was irksome for Saladin to accept Hossein's presence. He knew its significance. The telephone-call had been short but explicit. "Hossein arrives on the Alitalia flight from Rome, ten o'clock tomorrow morning. Be at the airport!"

"I accept full responsibility for what has happened," Saladin said stiffly.

Hossein shrugged. He lowered the window an inch, allowing the smoke to swirl out and picked his nose thoughtfully.

"You seem to have run this affair like a gangster. The Council deplores such methods. Your instructions were clear. There was to be no involvement with the local authorities. And what happens? Three deaths and this ridiculous business of a man's finger being amputated."

"The tip of a finger," Saladin corrected. "Pelham was asking for money. It was blackmail."

"Then why is he still alive?" Hossein threw his cigarette-butt into the rain.

Saladin chose his words carefully. His future and that of his comrades hung in the balance.

"We knew nothing about this diary until Pelham told us."

Hossein's fingers were stained with nicotine. He looked at them. "Where is the diary?"

They were nearing the end of the Chiswick flyover. It was the question that Saladin dreaded.

"It will be in my hands any moment. I pledge my word on it."

"Your report refers to an ex-policeman who is writing a book on the trial. Is this correct?"

"There will be no book written," Saladin answered. "Pelham has gained Raven's confidence."

The younger man grunted. "You say that the authorities have not been involved. How is this possible?"

Saladin joined the traffic for Hammersmith Broadway. "There have been no complaints by the police, no investigations. We know this for certain. The two women died as the result of an accident. The bookdealer committed suicide."

Hossein returned his attention to the end of his nose. "What has happened is disastrous. And it comes at the worst possible moment. The French are already searching diplomatic bags. The Italians and British will certainly follow. Your business here is terminated, Saladin. We cannot afford to lose credibility when we are fighting a war against prejudice. Half-a-million young men have died already."

"You pass harsh judgement, Hossein," said Saladin.

Hossein moved his thin shoulders. "It is the judgement of the Council, not mine. I return in three days' time. The diary must be in my hands before then, Raven and Pelham eliminated. Stop here!"

They were fifty yards from the Hyde Park Hotel. Hossein reached back for his bag.

He settled his coat round his shoulders. "You will receive instructions how to dispose of your assets. Do not come near my hotel or the embassy. A simple telephone-call will suffice. Do I make myself clear?"

"Quite clear," said Saladin. He was being dismissed like some servant.

Hossein slammed the car door and entered the hotel.

Saladin turned onto Queen's Gate and parked near the rear entrance to his apartment-building. Window faced window across deep airless wells. The corridors were painted a dark shade of green. He opened the door to his flat. He had been in the apartment for five years. Since then no stranger had put foot inside. Saladin was unknown in the block. The phone was listed under another name. He received no mail.

Saladin had first arrived in England with a bank-draft for half-a-million pounds and a diploma from a Montreal school of languages. He kept a drawer of translation work ostensibly in progress and used his typewriter daily. He came with a list of names supplied by Tehran. Two of these names were designated as essential. The first was Ali Reza doing a post-graduate course in the treatment of drug-addiction. The second was Sayed Nahavi, a student at the Harrington Drama Academy. The rest of the names and addresses were in various parts of the country. All had taken the oath of fidelity.

The telephone rang about one o'clock. It was Reza.

"Nahavi knows where Pelham is hiding!"

"Where are you speaking from?" Saladin asked quickly.

"We are at Dino's Restaurant, Gloucester Road."

"Come here immediately," Saladin ordered. "And use the back entrance."

He prepared the thick Persian coffee and placed three small cups on a beaten brass tray together with a bowl of raisin-stuffed almonds. Then he lit a cigarette and sat on a chair facing the front door. Minutes passed. The elevator doors opened and closed. A hand appeared through the flap of the letter-box. Saladin unlatched the door.

Two men stepped in, Reza wrapped in a wet raincoat, Nahavi wearing mud-spattered white trousers and a black leather jacket. He was a full six inches taller than either of the other men and wore an embroidered headband low on his ears and forehead. He hung his jacket on a hook and sniffed at the coffee with easy familiarity.

"Hossein is in London," Saladin announced. "I just drove him from the airport. To put it baldly, we have three days to find the diary and get rid of Pelham and Raven."

"Get rid of?" Reza repeated.

"Kill," said Saladin. "These are the Council's instructions."

Nahavi spooned sugar into his cup. "The Council is full of women. Hossein is a woman. I spit on them all."

"We have failed," answered Saladin. "Now the bill has come in. Each of us has to decide how much of that bill he is willing to pay. There are passports and money available for anyone who wants to leave now. It is up to us."

Reza was first to reply. "And you, Saladin, what do you do?"

"I have no choice," Saladin replied. "I stay."

"I stay," Reza echoed.

Nahavi's strong teeth crunched an almond. "My teachers tell me that I have a career full of promise. I stay."

They shook hands, breaking the tension. "Pelham!" said Saladin pointing at Nahavi.

The actor tilted his chair and removed his headband. "I've been twice to the flat and once to Putney since Pelham went missing. No luck at either place. This morning I drove to Fulham and Chelsea and made a few enquiries, places he used to frequent. No luck there either. I was just about to leave when suddenly there was Pelham, walking along Fulham Road with a bunch of flowers."

Saladin was leaning against the wall, his hands in his pockets. "Are you sure it was Pelham?"

The actor nodded. "I have seen him on six separate occasions. Remember, I took the pictures in Hamburg and Brussels. It was Pelham! He went into a club near Beaufort Street and came out a few minutes later without the flowers. He got on a bus to South Kensington and went into the Royal Bank of Scotland. It was easy to follow. I know him but he doesn't know me. He left the bank and entered a house on Draycott Place. I watched the place for half an hour. As far as I know he's still there."

Saladin came off the wall. "How about Raven?"

"I haven't seen him," answered Nahavi.

"He is still on the boat," said Reza. "I was there twice as I told you. The lights were on when I left and his car was in the cul-de-sac."

The actor yawned in the silence that followed. Saladin walked a few paces and turned.

"Helga Heumann was German. Suppose her diary is out of the country?"

Reza leaned forward. "You mean one of them knows where it is?"

"That is what we have always assumed," said Saladin. "It could be in Amsterdam. They could be preparing to go there."

Nahavi looked up from his fingernails. "The answer is simple. Let me go to see Pelham. I guarantee he will talk."

Saladin dismissed the suggestion. "That makes no sense. Raven was a detective. He will know how to procure false papers."

"Always we come back to Raven," the actor said sourly. "He must have a price."

"His price is our destruction. Pelham is his creature, I am sure of it. Concentrate on Pelham," Saladin urged. "What are his main interests?"

"Women and drink," the actor said promptly.

"Exactly. What sort of house is this where Pelham is staying?"

"A place for students and transients. Three houses are joined together."

"So we could rent a room?" asked Saladin.

Nahavi moved his shoulders. "I imagine so."

The idea took shape in Saladin's mind. "We need to know what Pelham is doing. We can be sure that he is acting in concert with Raven. We must know their plans. It has to be done subtly without Pelham realising what is happening. We need a woman we can trust." He looked at the others in turn.

The actor turned his mouth down. Reza refilled his coffee-cup. "There is a possibility," he said. "But also a problem. The woman I'm thinking of is an addict, an out-patient at the Clinic. She has a history of stealing prescription-forms from surgeries, that sort of thing. For the right reward she would do what she's told."

Nahavi made no secret of his feeling. "I trust no woman, least of all an addict."

Saladin ignored him. "Describe her," he said to Reza.

Reza thought for a moment. "She is in her thirties, divorced and living alone, attractive."

"Could you be sure of her?" Saladin insisted.

Reza lifted his hands. "I can be sure of her habit."

Saladin reached his decision. "Nahavi will rent a room where Pelham is staying. The woman will go there and wait. We have two options then. Pelham goes out at some stage, Nahavi follows. As soon as Pelham has settled somewhere Nahavi tells the woman. She then finds a way of approaching him. If he *doesn't* go out, the woman must knock on his door. In either case she must flatter him, sleep with him if necessary. It is essential that we know his plans without alarming him. She is a woman, she will know what to do. If this fails we have lost nothing. But we have to move quickly."

Reza lifted his hands again. "We can try. As you say, there is nothing to lose."

Saladin pushed the telephone at him. "Call her!"

Both men were quiet as Reza made his voice warm and comforting. "Mrs. Hammond? It's Doctor Reza from the Clinic. How are you? Yes, I know how depressed you have been and I may be able to help you."

He spoke in guarded tones at some length before putting the phone down.

"She'll do it. I have to go to her flat. I'll need a picture of Pelham."

Saladin pulled a bundle from a drawer. The picture he chose showed Pelham on the steps of Knightsbridge Crown Court talking to a group of reporters. He gave it to Reza.

"The first thing is to get the room," he said, looking at his watch. "Where does she live?"

"Sloane Avenue Mansions," said Reza.

"I can take you," said Nahavi. He slipped into his leather jacket and adjusted his headband. "I'll get the room while you see the woman."

Saladin accompanied them into the hallway. They exchanged embraces.

"I shall be here if you need me," said Saladin, and shut the door.

CHAPTER 9

Pelham opened his eyes, convinced that he hadn't slept. It was dark outside and he could hear the rain against the windows. He switched on the light. It was half-past six by his watch. He yawned, arching his back and staring at the ceiling. The thought of Raven disturbed him. He had always had a secret fear of violence and remembered the scene on the boat with misgiving.

He pulled on his trousers and splashed his face with cold water. Raven was due for a shock. Meanwhile there was no point in sitting in this crummy room, brooding. He donned his shirt and Raven's windbreaker and checked the cash in his pockets. There was enough for a few drinks. His passport, ticket, and the two hundred pounds were safe in the refrigerator. The idea of going back to Francesca's bar was tempting but he rejected it. The place would be full of people he knew.

He closed the curtains so that it was impossible to see in from outside. A smell of bacon frying hung in the landing. He paused on the steps in front of the street door. Cars parked on both sides narrowed the traffic to a single line of impatient drivers. The idea of Raven hanging around on a night like this was unlikely. In any case, he'd only be gone for an hour.

He turned the corner onto Milton Street. The wet pavement reflected the lights of a bar twenty yards away. The place was unknown to him. He pushed through the door and blinked hard, getting his bearings. Diffused light swirled on the ceiling, drifted like woodsmoke. There was a mural depicting nuns walking hand-in-hand through a hayfield. Chopin tinkled in hidden speakers. He took the only empty table and waited for service. It was some time before a woman swayed from the bar, dressed in a long black dress of some clinging material. Diamenté earrings dangled from her lobes and her enormous eyes stared from a dead-white face.

"Yes?" she asked bleakly.

"I'd like a Campari-and-soda," he said, looking up. "With a slice of lemon."

She turned away without answering and spoke to the girl behind the bar. Both women were dressed in identical fashion. Couples at the other tables were sitting very close together. After the first look nobody paid him any attention. He pulled out his cigarettes. By the time the match died in the ashtray he had the message. In spite of the slouched fedoras and design jackets there wasn't a man in the house apart from him. His reaction was mixed. Some of the girls were outstandingly beautiful. Time went by. The music was quiet, the whispering in the bar even quieter.

Pelham raised a hand. "Bartender! Am I allowed to ask what happened to my Campari-and-soda?"

The girl behind the bar plucked a bottle from a shelf and poured. Her colleague brought the glass to Pelham's table, her mouth disapproving.

"You forgot the lemon," he said.

She stalked back to the bar and returned with a slice of lemon on a saucer. She tipped it into his glass very carefully.

"Thank you," he smiled. One drink would be enough here.

A woman came through the entrance. She stood for a moment as Pelham had done, her eyes veiled as she surveyed the room. She appeared to be in her mid-thirties with brown hair reaching almost to her shoulders. She was wearing a green tailormade suit and five-inch heels. An elegant woman, he thought. And far too good for the likes of these trollops. She was halfway across the room when he realised she was heading straight for his table.

Her voice was quiet, her accent well-bred. "Do you mind if I share?"

He was on his feet quickly. "Please do! If you're expecting someone, may I offer a drink while you're waiting?"

"That would be kind. A tomato-juice if I may."

He relayed the request to the bar and studied her face. Grey eyes were set wide over a short straight nose. She was wearing coral nail-varnish and a scent that reminded him of Harriet Horne. There were no rings on her fingers. She lit a cigarette, holding her hair away from the flame with one hand. Her arrival had excited comment at the other tables. The waitress brought the drink.

"I don't want to be personal . . ." Pelham began.

"Why not?" she demurred. "You want to know what I'm doing in a lesbian bar. I could ask you the same question." She seemed to be mocking herself as well as him.

He shrugged. "My story's simple. I'm a visitor to London and this was the first bar I saw when I left the hotel. I'll admit it isn't exactly what I was looking for."

She gave him a slow easy smile, stirring the ice in her glass with a finger.

"My excuse is a little more complicated. In the first place I'm divorced and I live alone. Sometimes the rooms get too small for me. And then I saw you on the street when I was parking my car. I followed you in. You're an attractive man."

"Thank you," he said.

"And your manners are good."

He offered his hand. Her touch struck fire in his flesh.

"John Raven," he said. There was a perverse pleasure in using the name.

"Marina Hammond," she said. "I have a feeling that I've seen you before. Your face is familiar. Are you someone famous?"

"Nobody famous." he said.

"What do you do, Mister Raven?"

"Guess!" he grinned.

She moved round the table and sat on the couch beside him, looking him up and down.

"It's difficult. You could be a salesman of some kind. You've got that look of self-assurance."

"I'm a writer," he said. "I'm living in Germany and came over to see my agent."

"What sort of books do you write?"

"Suspense stories," he answered. "I'm working on one that's based on a court-trial."

Her fingers worked nervously. "Where do you live in Germany?"

"Do you know Düsseldorf?" He was breaking new ground and had to be careful.

She shook her head, her hair swinging with the movement.

"I'm staying with friends there," he added.

She played with the neck of her blouse. "And what are you doing alone?"

"Why is anyone alone?" he countered. "I'm out of touch with the scene here."

She swung a length of leg. Her stockings were seamed. "Which hotel are you in?"

"The Royal Court," he replied. He visualised her bedroom, sheets that smelled of her scent.

Her voice held a touch of sadness. "Here we are, two adult people in need of affection. Ships that pass in the night. What are we going to do about it, Mister Raven?"

"I'm not sure," he admitted. "And there is one small problem."

She touched his damaged hand, rekindling the blaze. "You're gay. That doesn't matter. I said affection. It covers a lot of ground."

"That isn't what I meant," he argued.

She rounded her mouth at him. "You mean you don't like men?"

"I like some of them. Why, don't you?"

Her throat bubbled laughter. "I'm sure we can work something out."

The suggestion stirred him strongly. It was suddenly important to show her what could be done with a responsive woman.

"The problem is that I have to be up very early in the morning."

She put her cigarettes and lighter in the green patent-leather handbag.

"No one's going to hold you captive, my friend. We can forget the whole idea if you like."

"I *want* it to happen," he said. "It's just that I have a plane to catch in the morning."

She took his cigarette from his grasp, dragged deep on it and destroyed it in the ashtray.

"Sloane Avenue Mansions. It's just round the corner. I'm on the second floor. Two-one-eight. We can't leave together. You'll just have to get wet. Fifteen minutes."

He walked by way of Draycott Place, looking up at his window as he passed. The light still shone behind the curtains.

A porter looked up from a desk as Pelham crossed the lobby. "Can I help you, sir?"

Pelham's thumb was on the elevator button. "I can manage, thanks."

The car rose to a discreetly-lit corridor where dried flowers spilled from alcoves. Two-one-eight was one of a pair at the end of the corridor. The dark varnished door was ajar. He stepped into the hallway and closed the door quietly.

"In here!" she called.

He followed her voice to a bedroom on his left. An oil-painting lit by a picture lamp stood on an easel. The artist had posed Marina Hammond standing in front of a mirror, one arm raised, her fingers deep in a maze of russet-brown hair.

She was sitting up naked in the wide bed, leaning against the wicker headboard. Her body was that of a twenty-year-old. Heavy drapes insulated the room from the sound of the traffic below. The walls and ceiling were matt-white. Polar bear rugs were strewn over the polished oak flooring. The bathroom door was open. A blue towelling robe was draped on the side of the tub.

Her voice was casual as though asking the time of a stranger. "Why did you lie to me in the bar?"

He felt the quick burn rise on his neck. "What the hell are you talking about?" he demanded.

"Oh, forget about it," she said impatiently. "Just get undressed."

The bed sank under his weight. "Not until you tell me what you mean."

She cradled her knees in her arms. "All that business about having to catch a plane in the morning. Why not just tell the truth. You fancy me enough to go to bed with but you don't want to spend the night here."

"I told you the truth," he replied. "I've got to be at Heathrow at eight o'clock in the morning. The plane leaves for Düsseldorf at nine-fifteen."

Her hand touched his cheek. "I forgive you."

He pulled off his clothes, aware of his sun-tanned body in the full-length mirror. He reached for the master-switch. The only light left burning was in the bathroom. New shadows lay across the bed. He rolled sideways, his lips moving from her armpits to her nipples. She stirred restlessly, pushing his head away. He moved on top of her, supporting his weight on his elbows, looking into her eyes. They were wide open and fathomless. She avoided his mouth and pulled him down, her cool hands resting lightly on his shoulders. Frustration fed lust as he sought response. But the intimate parts of her body seemed to reject him. He redoubled his efforts, indifferent now to her needs. His climax came and went quickly, leaving him with a sense of having been cheated. He swung himself from the bed and went into the bathroom.

She lay quite still as he put on his clothes.

"You know your trouble?" he said. "You're neurotic."

"Please go," she said quietly. "And make sure that the door's properly shut."

It was five minutes to nine as he crossed the lobby.

She waited until she heard the elevator start its descent. Then she stood in the tub, directing the needlespray over her body. There was no sense of defilement. Her only feeling was one of relief. She wrapped herself in the robe and picked up the phone.

"He's catching a plane for Düsseldorf in the morning. Nine-fifteen from Heathrow."

"Good work," said Reza.

She was beginning to sweat. She wiped her face on her sleeve. "I need something now. You promised."

"I have no time," he replied. "Someone will come to your flat in the morning. Good night, Mrs. Hammond."

The phone went dead in her hand. She leaned forward and took a folded strip of paper from a drawer in the dressing table. Tomorrow seemed a lifetime away. She took the piece of paper into the kitchen and emptied it onto a square of aluminium foil. She placed the foil on a gas-burner and held back her hair with both hands.

The foil curled at the edges and the white powder started to smolder. She bent low, dragging the fumes deep into her lungs. Her brain bombarded her senses with signals, soothing her jangling nerve-ends. She turned off the gas. Each movement now was mechanical. It was a great distance back to the bedroom. She lowered herself down on the pillows and turned out the lights. Her eyes closed under their own weight and she dozed in a dream, remote and beyond all intrusion.

CHAPTER 10

Raven pulled the curtains back and glanced down at the rented Renault. In spite of the downpour, the meter-beaters were already out. A parking-ticket was attached to the windshield. He dialled Patrick O'Callaghan's home number. The lawyer's voice was irate.

"And about time too! I've been leaving messages on your answering-machine since nine o'clock last night."

"I didn't sleep on the boat," said Raven. "I spent the night at the Cadogan Hotel. What do you have for me?"

"You're still going to Düsseldorf?"

Raven looked at his watch. It was five to nine. "In about four hours' time."

"I thought Kirstie and Maggie got back today."

"They do," said Raven. "Kirstie's coming to Düsseldorf with me." The prospect of breaking the news to his wife was something he preferred not to dwell upon.

"If you're worried about leaving her alone," said his friend, "she can stay here with us."

"She'll come with me," said Raven. He took a sheet of writing-paper from the desk. "OK, tell me!"

The man's name is Helmut von Brockdorf, Rechtsanwalt, 490 Oberkasslerstrasse, Düsseldorf. Telephone 54701 or 54702."

"Is he any good?" Raven asked.

"One of the best. An Honours degree at Bonn and two years at Harvard Law School. He's completely bilingual and there's something else. His father-in-law is a member of the Nord-

Rhein-Westfalen parliament. I had a long talk on the phone with him last night. He's willing to act for you."

"That's great, Patrick," said Raven. "What have you told him?"

"Pretty much everything. How you came to be mixed up in this business. The sort of person you are. None of it seemed to disturb him too much. It was Hector Stuart who put me on to him."

"Who's that?" asked Raven. The name was unknown to him.

"Someone I know. Von Brockdorf defended a friend of his on a drunk-and-driving offence. According to Hector, von Brockdorf's very anti-drugs. Something to do with a tragedy in his family. That made him an obvious choice. He's expecting you at his office at six o'clock tonight."

"I'll be there," promised Raven.

"If you can't make it for any reason, call him. He'll arrange another appointment. What have you done with Pelham?"

"He left on the nine-fifteen for Düsseldorf. I just checked with the desk at Heathrow. Look, Patrick, I have to get going. I'll call you later, and thanks for everything."

He paid his bill and went out to the rented car. The parking-ticket was tucked under a windshield-wiper and enclosed in a weatherproof plastic envelope. He dropped it down the nearest storm-grid. It was just before ten when he turned onto the slip-road to the airport. He found parking-space in the building opposite Terminal Two, carried his bag across the walkway and stood by the bank in the Arrival Hall. He glanced up at the display-screen as the letters and numerals dissolved and re-formed. OS 451 FROM VIENNA LANDED.

He hung over the rail, close to the exit. Kirstie and Maggie came from the Customs Hall, Maggie moving like some great cat on the prowl. She was taller than Kirstie by three or four inches and wearing a black velvet cape clasped with a hunk of amethyst over a white dress. Kirstie was in an Aquascutum raincoat worn with a sea-green beret. Both women were deeply sun-tanned.

Raven kissed each in turn and held his wife at arm's length before pulling her close again. The freckles across the bridge of her nose deepened in color. She wriggled free after a moment, a look of puzzlement invading her eyes.

"A suit and a tie, no less! What's going on?"

Raven gave the car-keys and parking-slip to the model. "I'm sorry to have to do this to you, darling, but Kirstie's coming to Düsseldorf with me. The car's up on the top floor. Call Avis when you've finished with it and they'll send someone round to collect. The bill's paid."

Kirstie swung round on him fiercely. "Hold on a minute! Maggie will do no such thing! What do you mean, coming to Düsseldorf with you? I just don't *believe* this!" she cried.

Raven dragged the bags out of the way. People were trying to get past. Maggie was looking extremely uncomfortable.

"I don't mind, Kirstie," she said. "I really don't. It's no hassle at all, I promise you."

"Why don't you let Maggie go?" said Raven. "You're embarrassing her." He caught the eye of a porter and loaded Maggie's bags on the trolley.

"Take this lady to the car-park. It's a black Renault on the top floor." He pushed some money into the man's hand.

Maggie touched Kirstie's sleeve. "Call me as soon as you get back." She blew a kiss at Raven and followed the porter.

Kirstie's eyes were as cold as Lake Ontario in March. "You're going to do this to me once too often," she warned.

He lifted her bag and started to walk, speaking over his shoulder. "If you'll give me a chance I'll explain."

She followed, tightlipped as they crossed to Terminal One. The girl at the BA desk checked the two tickets, tore out a couple of sheets and exchanged them for boarding-cards. Kirstie took hers in silence. They passed through passport control and the security-check. The Departure Hall was a scene of harassed confusion. Screaming children dashed through travellers bereft of direction. It was difficult to find a seat. Indian women in pajamas pushed broad-bottomed brooms over the Stayglo floor. Raven finally managed to claim a couple of hard vinyl chairs. They sat for almost an hour in silence.

"Are you going to carry on like this for long?" he asked, turning towards her.

She took off her beret and arranged her hair in her hand-mirror. "You don't have to explain," she said coldly. "It's something to do with that goddam girl, isn't it?"

"I'm sorry," he said.

"You're sorry!" she repeated. "Well, let me tell you something that you don't appear to realise, John. People are getting worried about you. Don't sneer! You're becoming totally self-ish. You don't think like a normal human being and you certainly don't act like one."

"Bullshit!" he said. "We must have had this discussion a hundred times. It's too late to expect me to change."

She snapped the clasp of her handbag on the mirror and brush.

"Too late for you to be less involved with things that don't concern you? Things that other people are better equipped to deal with than you are? You frighten me, John, and that's the truth!"

He resented the way she was able to strike where he was vulnerable. "It would help if you'd listen to me for once," he said stiffly.

She nodded her head. "You say listen. You don't seem to understand. What matters to me is our marriage. I don't want to see it go down the drain."

He took her hand in his, twisting the gold circles of her wedding ring. He had tried so often to explain how he felt and had failed.

"Everything you say is true. I know it. But it's not just the girl anymore. This thing has become a moral duty."

He told her some of what had happened. "Can't you see what I mean?" he pleaded. "These bastards think they're untouchable. They think they can kill people and get away with it. I can't let that happen, Kirstie."

She sighed. "I'm not going to be able to change you. I guess I've always known it. Maybe deep down I don't even want to. But I worry about you, darling. Does that seem so strange?"

"I've talked this thing through with Patrick," he argued. "The police are completely useless. The fact is I don't have one piece of real proof. Even Pelham's confession is useless without the people behind him. I have to get hold of this diary. It's as simple as that."

She sank her chin in cupped hands. "It's a horrible, horrible business and I do understand how you feel, darling. You're frustrated. What I don't understand is why this man Pelham's not in jail this very minute. Anyone else would have been. Come on, now, you know this is true!"

"I *need* him," Raven said patiently. "I need him in Germany. He's got to be where I can see him. Surely you can understand that?"

A voice spoke on the Tannoy. "British Airways announce the departure of Flight 750 to Düsseldorf. Passengers holding boarding cards should proceed to Gate 32!"

Kirstie came to her feet, and slung her cameras over her shoulder. "The thought of being in the same hotel as that monster makes me want to throw up."

He hefted their bags. "You won't *be* in the same hotel. You won't even see him, I promise."

"You're a hard man to live with," she said.

They followed the uniformed girl down the long ramp to the Boeing 737. They were airborne within minutes, climbing through rain and candyfloss clouds to a boundless world of bright sunshine. Raven lowered the blind on Kirstie's window.

She studied his face. "Let me ask you something, John. What exactly am I supposed to be doing in Düsseldorf?"

A vision of Helga slotted into his mind, her face as he last remembered it.

"I don't want you alone on the boat," he said quietly. "And I need you to give me strength."

She laughed. "I ask a simple question and get that sort of rubbishy answer. I suppose the truth is you can't stand sleeping alone any longer."

They were quiet for the rest of the journey, Kirstie reading her copy of *Vogue*. Lights came on in the overhead panel. A voice followed a chuckle on the speaker.

"This is your Captain! We are beginning our descent to Lohausen-Düsseldorf. The ground temperature is 8 degrees Centigrade, 46 degrees Fahrenheit. I'm afraid the weather is no better than it was in London. Rain with the promise of more to come."

Kirstie stirred and felt for her seatbelt. "I'll say this for you, lover, you bring me to the nicest places."

Peace had been made between them.

A cluster of brightly lit buildings rose from a waste of wet tarmac. The airplane made a neat three-point landing and screamed to a halt. It was quickly surrounded by men in yellow slickers. Steps were locked on, fore and aft. The passengers hurried into warmth and efficiency. Raven joined the EEC line for passport control. His wife still retained her Canadian citizenship. Their hotel was the Breidenbacher Hof. The room was comfortably furnished in the old-fashioned style. Dark waxed wood, heavy curtains with fringes, a bath-tub encased in mahogany. Taps with the gleam of silver.

"No plastic cups," Raven said, looking round. "No drinks-dispensers. Not even a television-set."

Kirstie threw her beret and coat on a chair, kicked off her shoes, and bounced on the bed.

"And the sheets smell of lavender. You're so *clever!*"

The telephone rang before he could answer. He picked up the handset. "Helmut von Brockdorf," said a voice. "I would like to speak to Mister John Raven, please."

"Speaking," said Raven. The German's English had the intonations of a Bostonian.

"Welcome to Düsseldorf, Mister Raven! I take it that you have my message from Mister O'Callaghan?"

"I have indeed," Raven answered. "Thank you for being so helpful. I understand I'm to come to your office at six."

"It would be better if you could make it earlier. I've been in touch with Herr Heumann. He will see us this evening. There are matters I'd like to discuss before we go there."

"When do you want me to come?" asked Raven. His wife was sitting up on the bed, watching him.

"Could you come now?" asked the lawyer. "My office is not far from your hotel. Ten minutes in a taxi. I believe your wife is with you?"

"Right here in the room," said Raven.

"Then please make my apologies for disturbing her stay," said the German. "Can I look forward to seeing you shortly?"

"I'm on my way." Raven replaced the phone. "That's the lawyer that Patrick found," he told Kirstie. "He wants me to go to his office now. Do you mind being left alone?"

She was back on the pillows, her hands behind her head. "I don't have much choice," she replied.

The switchboard connected him with the Hotel am Zoo. Herr Pelham was registered. Raven spoke to him.

"Stay where you are until I come to collect you. Have you got that firmly fixed in your mind?"

Pelham's voice was resigned. "Everything you tell me gets firmly fixed in my mind."

"Keep it that way," said Raven.

He used his wife's brush on his hair. "If things turn out as I hope, I'll be going to Paris from here. Want to come with me?"

She sat up straight again. "If you're serious, I'll call Madame Lambert and ask her to get the apartment ready. How long would we be staying?"

"Long enough to take care of some business," he said.

He sat down on the bed beside her, brought close by the thought of the Quai d'Anjou home she'd inherited from her brother. He remembered her fondly as a twenty-three-year-old newly arrived from Toronto, trailing around the advertising agencies with her portfolio. Invited for a drink, he had stayed for supper and the three days that followed.

She ruffled his freshly brushed hair. "Do you know what Maggie says about you? She says you're the one man in the world she'd be glad to meet in a dark alley. *Please* don't make me a widow!"

He brought her face close and kissed her lips. "I'll be back just as soon as I can."

The doorman had a cab waiting outside. It was still afternoon but the streetlamps were burning along Konigsallee, lighting the moss-covered statues and ornamental water. This was the commercial capital of Germany. Solid wealth buttressed its sophistication. The shop windows displayed luxury wares from Italy, France, and England.

The taxi turned left at the bottom of Konigsallee, passed through the green of the Hofgarten and over the Oberkasseler- brücke. The driver stopped in front of a glass-and-steel build- ing. Lights blazed on eighteen floors. The lobby was planned in American style with a coffee-shop, newsstand, and cigarstore. A soberly-dressed young man was standing by the elevators, watching the entrance. He came forward as Raven approached, speaking in formal English.

"Excuse me, sir. Are you Mister Raven?"

Raven nodded.

The young man smiled. "Doktor von Brockdorf is expecting you, sir!"

The elevator car rose swiftly, the indicator showing the speed of their ascent to the penthouse. They emerged into a flower-decked foyer with a panoramic sweep of plate glass. The city and river lay below in the rain. The young man tapped on a door.

"Mister Raven, Herr Doktor!"

Von Brockdorf rose from a pedestal desk, a bear of a man with a head of cropped reddish hair and smelling of cloves. His brown flannel suit was worn with a black knitted tie and gig-lamp spectacles with tinted lenses.

"Please sit down!" he said, pulling a chair for Raven.

There were no books or paintings in the room. Louvered windows controlled the amount of light that entered. The two men faced one another. Raven's dislike of lawyers went back to his childhood. A firm of family-solicitors had replaced his dead parents as guardians. It was an unhappy memory for Raven. Years with the police had hardened his antipathy to all branches of the legal profession. Patrick O'Callaghan was the only exception. Raven saw all others as vultures.

Von Brockdorf moved a framed photograph across the desk. "My son," he said quietly.

The likeness was of a teenager holding a hockey-stick on an ice-rink. The resemblance to the lawyer was striking.

"That was taken four years ago," said von Brockdorf. His expression was unchanged as he opened a drawer in his desk and produced a second photograph. It was difficult to accept that this was the same person. The young man was standing against a calibrated wall wearing some sort of uniform. Sunken eyes stared from a gaunt, hopeless face. Shock left Raven speechless.

The lawyer returned the picture to the drawer. "I wanted you to know why I agreed to help you. My son was a heroin addict. He started taking drugs at university. He dropped out after only a year. Of course we had no idea what was wrong at the time."

Raven found his voice. "Nobody does."

It was plain that the lawyer needed to talk. "Axel came back to Düsseldorf. I'm afraid I was harsh with him. His mother still reproaches me for it. He was our only child. Then strange things started to happen. Money went missing. Some of my wife's jewellery disappeared. Our maid gave notice and left, a woman who'd been with us for fourteen years. Then a forged check of mine was presented but the bank refused payment. Axel vanished. The next we heard, he'd been arrested in Basel.

He'd broken into a pharmacy, looking for drugs. He was sentenced to a year in prison. He died there last March." His expression saddened. "As you can imagine, the papers were full of it. Things have not been easy for my wife."

There was a dignity about the man, a courage in face of tragedy that stirred Raven's compassion.

"I'm sorry," he said. "I should never have come to you."

Von Brockdorf returned the framed picture to its original place. "I'm glad that you did. I had to tell you the facts."

He opened a folder of newspaper clippings. "The Düsseldorfer *Nachrichten* sent them over this morning. They had a reporter in London covering the trial. Mister O'Callaghan told me the rest of the story. He tells me that you were once a detective."

"That was a long time ago," Raven said. "My wife would tell you that I should never have been on the force. A lot of other people are of the same opinion. You'll know who I mean by Pelham?"

"The man who was charged with Helga Heumann. The man who was acquitted."

"Do you know that he's made a confession?"

Von Brockdorf inclined his head. "I know little about English law. But the principles are the same in most countries. A man cannot be tried twice for the same crime, surely."

"He's a self-confessed drugs-dealer," Raven answered. "A party to murder. But I need him, Doktor von Brockdorf. I may need him to get Helga's diary. He'll tell her father the truth if it's necessary. That's why he's here."

The lawyer held his spectacles to the light and polished the lenses.

"I'm afraid things may not be as simple as you think, Mister Raven. Let me tell you something about Herr Heumann. He is sixty-seven years old, a widower with a post office pension living alone outside Düsseldorf. You are not a father, I take it?"

"No children," said Raven.

Von Brockdorf resumed his spectacles. "Heumann is a practising Catholic whose daughter has disgraced his name. But that isn't the worst of it. Helga committed suicide. He can save his own soul but he can't save hers. This seems to be the clue to his thinking. He lives like a hermit, unable to face a world that he feels to be hostile and critical. My informant is someone who has known him for thirty years."

Raven's voice was exasperated. "But Helga was *driven* to suicide! That's the whole point of what I'm trying to prove! Surely the fact that his daughter was an innocent victim must matter to him?"

"He's from Sauerland," said von Brockdorf. "These people are set in their ways."

"Did you mention the diary to him?"

"Yes," said the lawyer. "I told him that someone was here from England, someone who believes that his daughter was innocent. I said that the diary would help. I said nothing about a book and I suggest that you do the same."

Raven moistened his lips. "But I *am* going to write it."

The lawyer shrugged. "That must be your decision. According to Heumann, Helga kept diaries for the last eight years. He has them all."

"I'm only interested in the one she sent from England in April. Pelham is part of it. I want him to look Herr Heumann in the face and ask for forgiveness."

"Suppose Pelham decides to make a run for it?"

"He won't," Raven said promptly. "There's nowhere for him to go. Not only that, he has no money."

"I have contacts in the Bundesgrenzschutz," said von Brockdorf, "I can have him stopped if he tries to run."

Raven gave it some thought. "Could you arrange things so that he's held if he shows up at a frontier without me?"

"I can try," said the lawyer. "I will need his full name."

"Piers Pelham," said Raven. "He's using a British Travel Document. He was born in Newbury, England, in 1955."

Von Brockdorf made a note. "Excuse me one moment."

The door closed behind him. The room was completely silent. Raven's confidence in the German was growing. His imagination spiraled into a vision of the Iranians still looking in London with no idea that time was running out for them.

Von Brockdorf returned looking pleased with himself. "My friends have just put Pelham through the computer. He has been in Germany four times before. He came in through Frankfort twice, once through Hamburg and once through Munich. I have his passport number." He glanced at a slip of paper in his hand. "822161E. This means that the document he is using now must be false."

"I know about that," said Raven. "The Iranians have his original passport. He had to lie to get this one."

"That's not our concern," said the lawyer. "It's enough to hold him while enquiries are made. He'll be stopped wherever he tries to leave Germany unless you are with him."

He came to his feet. "We'd better be thinking about making a move. It's a fairly long drive to where Heumann lives."

"May I call my wife?" Raven asked.

Von Brockdorf waved at the phone. "Help yourself."

It was a while before Kirstie answered. "Be quick, I'm in the bath. I'm standing here dripping all over the carpet."

Raven's voice buzzed with excitement. "I think we've cracked it, darling! Doktor von Brockdorf's driving me to see Helga's father. We shouldn't be long."

"I'll be waiting," she said.

Raven grinned at the lawyer. "She doesn't always approve, you'll have gathered."

Von Brockdorf closed the drawers in his desk. "I have to ask you this question, Mister Raven. Are you carrying a weapon of any kind?"

"Not even a penknife," said Raven.

"And the other man?"

"Don't worry about him," Raven answered.

The lawyer's car was a dark-green BMW with a radiophone bracketed under the dashboard. He drove up the ramp to the street with the windshield-wipers already working. Blurred lights traced the span of the bridge. Von Brockdorf slowed at the entrance to Shadowstrasse.

"How long are you planning to stay in Düsseldorf?"

"No longer than necessary, I'm afraid," said Raven. "I have people to see in Paris."

"A pity. I would have liked to show you both the Altstadt. It's our version of Montmartre and Soho rolled into one. It was flattened during the war but you know the Germans. They rebuilt it stone by stone from plans in the city archives."

"Were you in Düsseldorf during the war?"

The BMW surged forwards. "I spent the war years in a house that my parents owned in Winterberg. My father was in the army on the Eastern Front. Then the Americans came. Can you imagine. Until then I had never even seen a banana, didn't even know what it was. One of my sisters told me that you cooked it and ate it with salt. I was eight years old." He laughed at the memory.

Raven had the impression that the lawyer was talking to put him at ease. Streetcar tracks glistened in front. They were travelling along Grafenbergerallee. The lawyer's driving was conducted with a sort of disciplined aggression that allowed no quarter to those who disobeyed regulations. He turned the car left into a quiet residential area where linden trees lined the wet streets. The houses stood solid in well-kept gardens.

Raven moved suddenly, touching the lawyer's arm. "Take the first on your right!"

The lawyer followed instructions for the next five minutes, following a circuitous route that brought them back where they started.

"Pull over," said Raven. He pointed up at the rearview mirror. "We're being followed. A white Porsche. They've been on our tail for the last two miles."

Von Brockdorf was unconcerned. "The Criminal Police, Kripo inspectors. I asked for an escort."

The Porsche had stopped fifty yards behind. Raven took his eyes from the mirror.

"Do you mind telling me why, Doktor von Brockdorf?"

The lawyer took a clove from a small silver box and pouched it in his cheek.

"You should ask your friend Mister O'Callaghan."

"Why O'Callaghan?"

"He seems to think that you're in need of protection."

"Oh my God!" said Raven, shaking his head. There seemed no limit to the length that his friend was prepared to go. "You mean that the Düsseldorf police provide an escort for people like me?"

"When you fly do you buy insurance?"

Raven goggled with disbelief. "As a matter of fact, I do. My wife always insists on it."

"Then think of this as a form of insurance," the lawyer said easily. "I have friends in the Praesidium."

He put the car in action again. Rain dripped from the trees in a nearby driveway. The Porsche turned in behind them. Von Brockdorf stopped the BMW.

"Hotel am Zoo. I will wait in the car."

The lobby was small and cheerful. A girl with a ready smile greeted Raven from the Reception desk.

"Mister Pelham," he said.

She looked at the keyboard and nodded. "Number twelve. Shall I tell him that you are here, sir?"

"I'll surprise him," said Raven.

Pelham's room was halfway along a corridor. A strip of light showed at the bottom of the unlocked door. Raven turned the handle and stepped inside. Pelham was in an armchair watching television with the sound turned off. His windbreaker was on the bed. Raven went through the pockets, throwing whatever he found on the bed. Pelham's flight-ticket and travel document, a few D-marks and some English money. Raven counted more than £200.

"Where did you get this?" he asked.

"My mother gave it to me," said Pelham.

"On your feet!" ordered Raven.

He ran practised hands down Pelham's legs and patted his body. "OK," he said. "Put your jacket on. *Move!*"

Pelham's face reddened. "What's all this about? I thought we were on the same side."

"Never in a thousand years." Raven poked a finger into Pelham's chest. "We're going to see Helga's father. He may want to hear how you treated his daughter."

"You know what you are," said Pelham. "You're a bloody sadist!"

"And when we get there," said Raven, "you only speak when you're spoken to."

He placed his hand in the small of Pelham's back and they went down the stairs. The girl at the desk looked up.

"Will you be eating in the hotel tonight, Mister Pelham?"

"He doesn't know," Raven said, smiling.

Von Brockdorf turned his head as Pelham got into the rear seat. There were no introductions. They went left at the end of Grafenbergerallee onto Graf Reckestrasse. Raven could see the Porsche following, the driver allowing other vehicles to come between the two cars and accelerating whenever it was necessary to maintain his distance. A sports complex showed up on the right. A few forlorn lamps shone on wet grass and a deserted stadium. There were no houses, just fields and beyond these the forest. Bends in the road put the Porsche out-of-sight occasionally but the distinctive noise of its engine was always there. The forest began to crowd in on the road. Fir-trees showed in the beam from the headlamps. Watery lights appeared outside an inn. Music came from behind curtained windows. The lawyer swung off the road and unfastened his seatbelt.

"I must ask directions. I'll be back in a moment."

He ran towards the entrance, protecting his head from the rain with a newspaper. Pelham peered through the back window.

"There's a car following us," he said anxiously. "They've just put their lights out."

"Face your front and shut up!" ordered Raven.

Von Brockdorf hurried back to his seat. "Another five kilometers."

The Porsche lights came on as the BMW drove off.

The only sounds came from the motor, the windshield-wipers, and tyres. A faint glow showed ahead and the hardtop came to an abrupt end. They stopped on the edge of a clearing in the forest. In front of them was a sawmill and drying-sheds. A solitary lamp hung outside. A parked tractor had sunk deep in the sawdust and mud. The ground was covered with a network of duckboards. There were two houses, one on each side of the clearing.

Von Brockdorf pointed at the one on the left. "That's where Heumann lives. He rents it from the owner of the sawmill."

Raven lowered his window. Mud bubbled under the onslaught of rain like larva in a crater. An old Volkswagen was parked at the side of the timber-and-plaster home. The place was in darkness and shuttered.

"He's in there," said the lawyer. He spat the chewed clove through the open window and pouched a replacement.

The Porsche was out of sight beyond the last bend. There was no way of taking the BMW closer to Heumann's house. Von Brockdorf turned up his trouser bottoms.

"We'll just have to run for it."

The other two followed suit, each taking his own route. Raven moved awkwardly, slipping on the greasy duckboards. He was last to arrive. Von Brockdorf dried his spectacles and lifted the heavy door knocker. The crash echoed back from the trees. A dog barked in the house opposite. The three men waited uncertainly, water gurgling in the gutters above. The door scraped open. A grey-haired man surveyed them from deepset eyes in a face the colour of cheese. He wore knickerbockers, woollen stockings and heavy boots, and a highnecked jacket.

"Von Brockdorf," the lawyer said.

Heumann led them over fiber matting laid on stone-flags to a room at the back of the house. A log burned in an open fireplace. A copper kettle stood in the hearth nearby. The room was sparsely furnished with a few chairs, a bench against the whitewashed wall, and a table. A Black Forest clock ticked on the mantel. There was a telephone and a television-set.

A neatly-made bed showed through an open door beyond the fireplace. A tortured image of Christ on the Cross hung above the bed.

Heumann said something in German. His voice was unexpectedly frail. Von Brockdorf pointed at Raven. Pelham was on the bench, keeping a low profile. Heumann's boots creaked as he came nearer Raven. He peered down, stoop-shouldered, and turned to the lawyer again.

Von Brockdorf translated. "He wants to know what your interest is in his daughter. I've already told him but he wants to hear it from you. Be patient."

Heumann waited, his deepset eyes never leaving Raven's face.

"Tell him that I'm sure that his daughter was innocent," Raven said. "Tell him she was betrayed by the man she trusted."

A match flared as Pelham lit a cigarette. He smoked nervously, looking down at the floor. After the initial inspection Heumann had completely ignored him. Raven had the impression that the German had no idea who Pelham was. Heumann spoke again.

Von Brockdorf was standing close to the fire, his trouser-legs steaming.

"He's asking if you're a Catholic."

"Tell him yes but a bad one," said Raven.

Heumann put a log on the fire. Sparks flew in the smoke-blackened chimneypiece. His voice was barely audible.

"He wants to know why you need Helga's diaries," said the lawyer. His eyes signalled caution.

Raven cleared his throat. "Just the one she sent from London. Tell him I have to see it. There are things that can clear

Helga's name. Things that can help convict the men who are responsible for her death."

Heumann listened as though each word was precious. The fire collapsed in the sudden silence. Pelham seemed locked in some dark corner of his own mind. Heumann dragged his way to the table. He opened a drawer and turned, holding a small brown paper parcel. The knots in the twine were still sealed with green wax. Heumann looked from Raven to von Brockdorf before handing the parcel to the lawyer. Von Brockdorf pushed it into his jacket pocket. Heumann carried the table-drawer to the fireplace. It was crammed with diaries of all shapes and colors. He tossed them onto the flames. His voice sounded close to breaking-point.

"He says he's glad that his daughter found a friend," said the lawyer. "He thanks you. He wants us to go."

They made their way to the front door. Heumann opened it, an old and defeated man who still retained dignity.

"Auf Wiedersehen, meine Herren!"

The door scraped shut and the bolt rattled home firmly. The three men stood side by side, sheltering beneath the overhang. Raven was moved to sympathy.

"There can't be much left for a man like that," he said.

The lawyer turned up his collar. "Not very much."

A hundred yards of slush lay between them and the BMW. "We should have left the lights on," said Raven.

"Standing here won't make things any better." The lawyer slipped his spectacles in his pocket.

They ran through the rain, Pelham first, von Brockdorf last. The duckboards sank beneath Pelham's weight but Raven was committed to follow. His feet slipped as he moved. The head-lamps came on when they were twenty yards from the car. The front doors opened. There was a brief glimpse of two men wearing crash-helmets and black oilskins. Each man held a gun in his hand.

Raven knew who they were, instinctively. Pelham's look confirmed the hunch. Pelham was first to react, putting his full weight against Raven's chest and sending him spinning away from the light. Pelham's voice screamed back from the forest.

"Run for it."

Raven slithered towards the trees, Pelham close behind. The Iranians leaned on the roof and took careful aim. Raven dropped flat as two shots rang out. A bullet furrowed the mud near his neck. The second blew Pelham's brainpan asunder. He stood in the glare of the headlamps for a fraction of a second, brain matter and blood oozing from the exit hole in his forehead. Then he dropped like a pole-axed steer. Raven lay perfectly still, his body and face pressed into the mire. Footsteps squelched by. He heard the two men speaking in Farsi as they bent over Pelham. A series of freeze-frames followed. A woman screaming through the bark of a dog, machinegun fire rattling from the bend in the road. Raven retracted his head like a tortoise. The Iranians were lying in the mud close to Pelham. The two detectives splashed into the clearing, smoke dribbling from the mouths of their sub-machineguns. They were young, hatless, and wet. The door opened in the house on the right. A man and woman stood framed in the light. The dog behind was still barking.

One of the detectives ran forwards, brandishing his gun.

"*Tur zu!*" he shouted.

The door was slammed shut. The light in the hallway went out. There was no reaction from Heumann's house. Raven found himself lifted in a bear hug. Von Brockdorf peered through his wet spectacles.

"You are all right?" he asked.

One of the detectives was trotting towards the sawmill, gun at the ready, looking at the ground as he went. His companion bent over the three prostrate bodies and came across to von Brockdorf.

"*Sie sind todt alle drei, Herr Doktor.*"

The lawyer wrapped a heavy arm around Raven and helped him into the car. He wiped Raven's face with a handkerchief.

"Take off your things, your trousers as well."

Raven emptied his pockets and threw his clothes on the back seat. The lawyer opened the trunk and returned with a travelling-rug. "Wrap yourself in this. We'll get your stuff cleaned up later. They're dead, all three of them."

Raven closed his eyes. When he opened them again it was in response to a shout. One of the detectives was wheeling a motor cycle into the clearing. He propped the machine against the wall of the sawmill, had a brief word with the lawyer, and joined his companion. Both detectives walked off towards the police-car.

"The motor cycle is registered in Düsseldorf," said the lawyer. "They were here for some time before we arrived. The engine is cold."

He used the radiophone, speaking in German. "My father-in-law," said von Brockdorf. "He will help. I have asked for an ambulance. The officers will stay here."

Raven stared across the sea of mud. Someone had covered Pelham's head with the windbreaker. Raven pushed up the window. Pelham had saved his life. An involuntary movement perhaps, prompted by instinct, but the thought persisted.

"Pelham must have told them," he said. "He couldn't keep his word even to himself."

"That's something we'll never know." The lawyer turned the ignition key. "We're going to the Praesidium. The District-Attorney's a friend. For the time being, I'll take care of the diary."

It was difficult for Raven to control his voice. "Those bastards would have killed the three of us."

"Best not to think about it." The lawyer turned the BMW in a tight circle and waved as they passed the Porsche.

Von Brockdorf drove fast, his eyes fixed on the road ahead. "What happens now?" Raven asked suddenly.

The lawyer waited for the traffic-signals to change. "Inspectors of the Criminal Police shot dead two foreigners in the line of duty tonight. These men were suspected of dealing in drugs and had just killed a British tourist. Isn't that what took place?"

Raven looked at the radiophone. "I should call my wife."

"Don't do it, take my advice," warned the lawyer. "Wait until we've seen the DA. It's essential that you get your story right. You won't be under pressure but you will be on record."

Raven huddled under the travelling-rug. "I'm not quite sure what you mean by my story."

They were in the city now, travelling north on Grafenberger-allee. The lawyer reduced speed.

"It's common knowledge that you were a juror at Helga's trial. You believed in her innocence. You came to Düsseldorf hoping that Helga's father would help you establish it. But Heumann refused. He's a man with a private grief. His daughter is dead and this is how he wants to leave it. There *is* no diary."

"Suppose Heumann says otherwise?"

"He won't," von Brockdorf said with assurance. "And stop worrying about the diary. My secretary is bilingual and completely trustworthy. You'll have a translation before you leave in the morning."

A weight settled on Raven's shoulders. "Pelham will have to be buried. Someone's going to have to tell his mother."

"One thing at a time," said the lawyer. He turned left off Shadowstrasse into a neighbourhood of government buildings. The lawyer drove onto the forecourt and gathered Raven's clothing from the back seat.

"Don't be self-conscious. They're used to seeing strange things."

Raven knotted the rug round his middle. A sentry at the top of the entrance steps saluted, recognising von Brockdorf. The two men crossed the marble entrance-hall. None of the people passing gave them a second look. There was a sign on a door: OBERSTAATSANWALT FRAU INGEBORG JUNIUS.

The lawyer knocked once and pushed Raven into the room. A tall woman in her forties rose to greet them. Her pale blond

hair was coiled on her neck and she wore a black tailored suit
with a white silk shirt. Von Brockdorf kissed her hand.

"Gruss, liebe Ingeborg!"

Their German was too rapid for Raven to follow but he
heard his name mentioned. He stood uncomfortably, the car-
rug hanging from his waist. His shoes and socks were still wet.

"Please do sit down, Mister Raven!"

The District-Attorney's English was fluent. She pressed a
buzzer and a girl came into the room. She took Raven's
clothes, including his socks and shoes.

The District-Attorney smiled reassuringly. "We will make
sure that you leave here looking the perfect English gentleman."

The room was like any other law-office. Rows of files, legal
tomes, a battery of telephones, and a computer-screen. Raven
tucked the rug round his hairy legs. Von Brockdorf took a
cheroot from a box on the desk. His own clothes were mud-
spattered but he seemed unaware of it.

"Frau Junius would like to ask you some questions," he said.

The District-Attorney lifted her head from the papers in
front of her and gave her attention to Raven.

"You must tell me, please, if anything that I say is not correct. You are Mister John Raven, a British subject, staying with
your wife in the Breidenbacher Hof Hotel here in Düsseldorf.
Your wife is Canadian."

"That's right," said Raven.

"And Doktor von Brockdorf is your legal adviser in Germany."

Raven had been trained not to volunteer information but he
made an exception.

"Doktor von Brockdorf was recommended by my lawyer in
England, Patrick O'Callaghan."

Frau Junius studied Raven's face. A small pulse beat in her
shapely neck.

"Do you know the names Saladin or Reza?"

Raven sneaked a look at the lawyer. Von Brockdorf was polishing his spectacles.

"I know both these names by repute," Raven said guardedly.

"Herr Heumann?"

Raven shrugged. "I was a juror at his daughter's trial in London. She was accused of being involved in drugs offences. She was convicted and committed suicide shortly after her sentence. I believed that she was innocent. I still do. I came to Düsseldorf hoping that her father would help me to prove it."

"Why should you want to do that, Mister Raven?"

Once again, von Brockdorf gave him no help. "I believe in what's right," he said. It was weak but the best he could do.

The District-Attorney's voice had a lulling quality about it.

"Doktor von Brockdorf accompanied you to Herr Heumann's house?"

"He did," Raven agreed. "He called me at the hotel and I went to his office. Later on we went to see Herr Heumann."

"There was a third man with you. Who was he?"

This time von Brockdorf met Raven's glance. "An Englishman called Piers Pelham," Raven answered. "He lived for a while with Helga. He was tried on the same charge but acquitted."

"And why was Mister Pelham in Düsseldorf?"

Raven shuffled his bare feet. "I brought him here. I thought it was opportune. I wanted Herr Heumann to see the man who had treated his daughter so badly."

"But *why?*" Frau Junius persisted. "How could that serve your purpose?"

"I wanted Herr Heumann to see the kind of man Pelham was, a man with no conscience. I thought it might encourage Herr Heumann to tell me more about Helga. I was wrong as things turned out. Herr Heumann made his position clear. His daughter was dead and that was an end to it. I respected his wishes."

The District-Attorney made a note on her pad. "You say

that Mister Pelham was acquitted of the charge he faced. So
you would say that an innocent man was murdered tonight?"

Raven lifted his head. Words were being put into his mouth.
"He was murdered, yes."

"Helga had been convicted of offences involving a large sum
of money. You say you know who was really responsible?"

Raven nodded. "Your detectives killed them tonight, Frau
Junius."

The District-Attorney rose, smiling. She opened the door to
an adjoining room.

"If you'll wait in there, Gunilla will bring your clothes very
shortly."

The door closed, leaving Raven alone in a room with apricot
curtains hiding the ugliness of the windows. Wall-hung units
were filled with novels and bowls of pot-pourri. A Siamese cat
lay asleep on the carpet. Ten minutes passed and the secretary
came into the room, carrying Raven's clothing. She was no
more than twenty and wearing a yellow dress that set off her
crow-black hair. She held up each article for his inspection.
The mud had been cleaned from his suit. The fabric was still
warm from a steam-iron. His shoes had been polished. The
secretary turned away, opening a panel in the wall as he started
to dress.

"How do you like your coffee, Mister Raven?"

He felt better with clothes on. "Cream and sugar if you have
them, please."

The coffee was served in a handpainted earthenware mug
with flecks of chocolate floating on top. She folded the car-rug
neatly.

"Do you think I could make a call to my wife?" Raven
asked, pointing to the telephone on the desk.

"But of course!" she said quickly.

The cat wreathed through his legs as he dialled the hotel
number.

"And not before time!" Kirstie said. "Where on earth are
you?"

"Police-headquarters," he said. "There's been some trouble. Pelham got shot. He's dead."

Her voice sounded shocked. "Oh my God! Are you all right?" she asked quickly.

"I've been better," he admitted. The secretary was washing his mug in the alcove. "Look, I'm not sure how long this is going to take, darling. I'm with von Brockdorf in the District-Attorney's office."

"Where are you *exactly?*" she demanded. "I want the address."

"Don't you come here," he warned. "Everything's under control. You coming here will only complicate matters."

The secretary opened the door to the District-Attorney's office. "Frau Junius is waiting for you, Mister Raven."

Kirstie's voice took on an edge. "Who is that woman you're with?"

"I'll call you in half an hour," he said quickly. "Just stay where you are!"

The cat followed Raven and jumped onto the District-Attorney's lap.

"That looks *much* better," she said, looking at Raven.

A trolley bearing an electronic typewriter had been wheeled into the office. A girl wearing earphones was sitting behind it. A microphone stood on the desk. Raven sat down. Von Brockdorf spoke into the microphone. The typist's fingers moved quickly, following his German. Raven kept his eyes on the cat. Its tail lashed as Frau Junius kneaded the fur on its neck. When von Brockdorf concluded his speech, the typist gave him a sheaf of papers. He closed the door behind her, read through the typescript, and put the two copies in front of the District-Attorney.

"This is your statement," he said to Raven. "I'm not going to translate word for word, but this is the gist of it. The statement starts with the usual preamble. Your name, nationality, and so forth. You attest that you were a juror at Helga's trial. A majority verdict found her guilty. You were in opposition.

Enquiries that you made shortly afterwards led you to believe that Iranians had been responsible for the importation of the drugs concerned. You came to Düsseldorf to see Heumann, accompanied by Piers Pelham who had been Helga's lover. He had been charged with the same offence but was acquitted. Your reason for seeing Herr Heumann was to seek his help in proving his daughter's innocence. He took the view that no good could come in reopening the circumstances of his daughter's conviction and you left.

"To the best of your knowledge you had never seen either of your assailants before today. You further affirm that one of these men shot a pistol at Pelham, killing him on the spot. The other man also fired at you with a pistol but missed. You have been told that both these men were Iranians. The only reason that you can give for this murderous assault is that these criminals knew about your enquiries in London. You are an ex-Detective-Inspector for New Scotland Yard."

The lawyer got rid of the frog in his throat.

"You further affirm that you were able to see officers of the Criminal Police respond to the attack on you with machinegun fire. You have been told that both Iranians are dead. It is your intention to leave Germany tomorrow morning without prejudice to any action that the authorities here may wish to institute. You hold yourself ready to return to this country should this be deemed necessary for the purpose of justice. OK?"

"OK," said Raven, resisting the impulse to smile. Maybe this was what he's always meant by expediency.

"Sign here!" The lawyer offered his pen.

Raven affixed his signature to both copies of the document. Von Brockdorf's endorsement followed. The District-Attorney lowered a seal on all six pages and added her own signature.

"Danke sehr, Frau Oberstaatsanwalt," von Brockdorf said formally. She rose, dislodging the cat and smiled at each man in turn.

"Have a safe journey home, Mister Raven."

He followed the lawyer outside. The rain was sweet on his

face. He threw the rug on the back seat and took his place beside the lawyer.

"It's all over," the lawyer said. "You'll hear no more."

Raven reached into the glove-compartment for his Gitanes. "You mean three men have died and that's it?"

The lawyer started the motor. "The detectives have made their report. It is fortunate that we were there to witness what happened. It puts the incident in proper perspective."

Raven released a mouthful of smoke as the BMW moved forwards.

"They wouldn't appreciate your style at the Yard."

The lawyer cocked his head. "Does that mean they are not on the side of justice?"

Raven detected the irony. "They wouldn't be able to handle you," he said, grinning.

"Then it's just as well that we don't have to worry about them," the lawyer said briskly.

They turned right onto Konigsallee. The lawyer pulled into a space in front of the hotel.

Raven put the question on impulse. "What do you know about the US Federal Narcotics Service?"

Von Brockdorf moved his thick shoulders. "Isn't it something like Interpol?"

"Something like that," said Raven. The hotel lobby was a peaceful oasis after the earlier violence. "They've got agents all over the place. Europe, the Far East, South America. Anywhere that there's a market in drugs. The point is, when they talk, people listen."

The lawyer's face was curious in the light from the hotel entrance.

"What about them?" he asked.

"I'm going to see them in Paris," said Raven. "What I want to know from you is how much can I say of what happened here?"

The doorman was coming from the lobby under an enormous, striped umbrella. Von Brockdorf removed the car-keys.

"There's something that you should get perfectly clear in your head, Mister Raven. Nothing that happened tonight was morally or legally wrong. *Nothing,*" he emphasized.

He handed the keys to the doorman.

"I didn't mean that there was," said Raven. "I was asking a question."

Von Brockdorf checked his pockets and smiled. "If you feel it is right to talk to these people then that is what you must do."

"Come in and meet my wife," said Raven.

They ducked under the doorman's umbrella and entered order and perfumed elegance. Kirstie and Raven saw one another at the same moment. She hurried towards him, tawny-haired and sun-tanned. Her eyes dwelt briefly on her husband then she turned to the lawyer.

"Doktor von Brockdorf," said Raven. "My wife Kirstie."

The lawyer took her hand between his palms. "You must not fear for your husband, Mrs. Raven. I promise sincerely, it is all over. You must try to forget these things."

"Forget?" Her face showed what she felt as always. "Knowing John I'm sure that it could have been worse. Thank God you were with him. Won't you please stay and have something to eat with us?"

The lawyer released her hand. "There is nothing that I should like better but there are things I must do at the office."

Kirstie's eyes widened as the lawyer showed her the registered parcel.

"Helga's diary," said Raven. He wanted her to share in his triumph. "Doktor von Brockdorf's having it translated."

"You'll have it tomorrow morning," promised the lawyer. "Call me at home or at the office as soon as you have made your travel-arrangements. I will drive you to the airport. Now, good night to you both!"

They watched his broad back disappear through the revolving door.

"I like that man!" Kirstie said suddenly.

"I noticed," said Raven.

She fluttered her eyelashes at him. "Don't tell me you're jealous!"

He took her arm. "I'm jealous. Let's tell them to send a meal up to the room."

She planted both feet firmly. "I have been walking up and down that room for over three hours, worrying myself sick about you. Now I want to sit down at a table with candles and flowers and ask myself what the hell I ever saw in you."

"I was your Young Lochinvar home from the wars," he said. "Let's see about the tickets before we eat." He steered her towards the travel-bureau.

"I'd like two seats to Paris tomorrow morning," he said to the girl on duty.

She ran her scarlet-tipped nail down the flight schedule "Air France at nine-ten, sir?"

"Perfect," he said.

She punched a computer button and viewed the result on the screen. "No problem. Check in at Lohausen half-an-hour before takeoff. Arrival time is ten-fifteen Charles de Gaulle. How do you wish to pay, sir?"

He placed a credit card in front of her. She took the details and processed two tickets.

"Have a good flight!"

The restaurant-manager led Kirstie and Raven to a table. Raven narrowed his nose as a chafing dish went by.

"These Germans like their game high. That must be near walking."

"The man's waiting to take your order," said Kirstie. "I'll be happy with a steak and salad."

"I thought this was supposed to be a celebration," Raven objected.

"Oh, but indeed it is," she said winsomely. "Any time I get to spend the night with Young Lochinvar is a cause for celebration."

He ordered roast duckling for himself and a bottle of Ayala.

He shifted the flower-arrangement the better to see his wife and placed both elbows on the table.

She met his inspection coolly.

"OK, what is it?" he asked.

She glanced up from the flame of her lighter. "I'm waiting for the speech from the balcony. The one where you announce that this was your last glorious exploit."

He took his elbows away, one after the other. "That's precisely what it would have been, Kirstie. We're sitting here as though nothing had happened."

"Well, tell me about it," she invited, reaching across for his hand.

By the time he finished, Kirstie had smoked three cigarettes and the meal had been served.

"Thank God we go home tomorrow," she said.

Raven looked at her with tenderness. Faced with the death of a much-loved brother, she was capable of bravery. She showed blind and belligerent defence of her friends. But her concern for him was something special.

"Pelham saved my life tonight," he said. "And I'll never know why."

The smoke from her cigarette drifted between them. "The world's a better place without him as far as I'm concerned. I'm sorry but that's the way it is, darling."

"Maybe he had regrets. Anything's possible."

Kirstie refused the suggestion. "Did he have regrets when he moved that dope? Did he have regrets when those girls died? The man was a monster!"

"Someone will have to tell his mother," he said. "I'm going to offer to pay for his funeral."

"Of course." Her tone was devoid of sarcasm. "There are so many things about you that I don't understand."

It was true. It had always been true since the day they met. And there was no way that he could change things.

"Isn't it *possible?*" he said to her. "Isn't it possible that Pelham knew he was saving my life?"

"You're asking me and the answer is no," she said flatly. "I wouldn't give it a second thought. You're alive and that's all that matters."

Their appetites had evaporated and they left the table with the meal barely touched, the bottle of wine half empty. He slackened pace as they crossed the lobby. Someone was playing piano in the bar.

"You want a nightcap?" he suggested. "Something to cheer us up? I'll join you in a minute. There's a phone-call I have to make."

She shook her head, pointing at the couch where she had been sitting.

"I'll wait for you there."

He walked across to the phone-booths. An operator found the number. A man's voice came on the line.

"Federal Narcotics Bureau. Duty-Officer speaking."

"My name is John Raven and I'm speaking from Germany. I'd like an appointment to see one of your officers in Paris some time tomorrow afternoon." The conversation was sure to be taped.

"Are you able to give me some idea of the nature of your enquiry, Mister Raven?"

"It isn't an enquiry," he said. "I have information about drugs that should be of interest to you. That's all I'm prepared to say at the moment."

He waited as a hand was laid over the mouthpiece at the other end. The voice returned.

"Are you familiar with Paris, Mister Raven?"

"We have a home there."

"We're on Rue Lincoln, number thirty-six. Can you make three o'clock?"

"I'll be there," Raven promised.

"You'll find a bell and our name on the outer door. Someone will let you in. May I ask your nationality, Mister Raven?"

"I'm British." He gave them a few more facts to feed into

the computer. "My address in Paris is 35 Quai d'Anjou. The phone number is 554-9725."

He was halfway across the lobby when the girl at the desk caught his eye.

"We have a call for you, Mister Raven! Where do you wish to take it?"

Raven hurried back to the booth. Von Brockdorf's voice was wary. "Can your wife hear what I'm saying?"

Raven glanced through the glass. "No, she's sitting across the lobby."

"Then listen to me carefully. I'm still in my office. I've just been speaking to Frau Junius. The Iranians flew into Frankfurt yesterday. That's not all. There was a third man with them. The police have the name he is using but so far they've been unable to trace his movements. Have you made your travel-arrangements?"

"Yes. Air France, nine-ten from Lohausen." Raven scanned the crowded lobby with a new premonition of danger.

"Frau Junius wants me to assure you that there is no cause for alarm but we cannot afford to take chances."

Kirstie was looking in Raven's direction. He waved a hand.

"I'm concerned about my wife," he said. "Maybe we should get out tonight?"

"Don't do that!" the lawyer said sharply. "Precautions are being taken. The police are redoubling their efforts and mounting a special security check at Lohausen. You will board the airplane after the other passengers. I'll pick you up at the hotel, eight o'clock, sharp."

"You won't forget the diary?" It was never far from his thoughts.

"My secretary has taken it home. I'll pick it up on my way to you in the morning. Good night, Mister Raven."

Raven stopped at Reception. "I'd like to pay my bill now. We'll be leaving early tomorrow."

Kirstie lay in his arms in the darkness, her face on his chest. "Who was that on the phone before?"

"Von Brockdorf. We're getting VIP treatment at the airport."

"That's nice," she said dreamily. Her body suddenly stiffened. "What do you mean, VIP treatment?"

He held her a little tighter. "Some joker's on the loose and they think it's another Iranian. Try to get some sleep."

He kissed her mouth and they lay close like spoons.

The phone rang at a quarter to seven. Raven reached for it.

"Good morning, sir. This is your alarm-call. Breakfast will be served in your room in fifteen minutes."

He switched on the lamp. It was still raining outside. Daylight showed grey and forbidding. Kirstie was hidden under the sheet. He uncovered her face.

"Time to get up, sleepyhead!"

He had finished shaving when a tap came on the door. He carried the breakfast tray to the table. Kirstie had taken his place in the bathroom and was standing in front of the make-up mirror. She came into the bedroom, holding a lip-printed tissue. She lifted the cover on the breakfast tray and made a face.

"Sausages, eggs! At this time of the morning?"

He took his coffee into the bathroom. She had a model's knack of snatching her clothes on the run and dressing for the street in five minutes flat. By the time he came out, the two bags were packed and she was attending to her nails.

"I was thinking about that woman," she said. "I mean Pelham's mother."

He took one last look round the room. "I'll ask von Brockdorf to call her. I don't want to be the one who breaks the news."

The lobby was deserted except for a couple of Turkish cleaners. Raven and Kirstie took seats on a couch and waited. Von Brockdorf came just before eight wearing a stone-grey raincoat and a velour hat with a feather. His cheeks had been honed over the faded sun-tan. He greeted them hurriedly and picked up Kirstie's bag. They followed him out to the BMW. Kirstie sat in the back. The lawyer bullied his way into the early-morning traffic.

"You remembered the diary?" Raven asked anxiously.

Von Brockdorf took a hand off the wheel and tapped an inside packet.

"About Pelham's mother," said Raven. "Could you do me a favour and break the news? I don't have the stomach for that sort of thing anymore. The address is Palmerston Mansions, King's Road, London SW3."

"I'll take care of it," promised von Brockdorf. "There'll be no problem getting the body released."

They lapsed into silence, travelling fast along the Kennedy Freeway. A police Porsche had drawn into their wake. Raven looked in the rearview mirror. The crew was a different one from the night before. The dome-light was flashing but the syren was mute. The two cars turned into the vortex of Danzigerplatz and were spewed out on the road to the airport.

FLUGHAFEN DÜSSELDORF

They drove onto the approach road and forked away from the main terminal buildings. A gate in the razorwire fence barred the way. A couple of security guards in white slickers approached the BMW, one on each side. One of them acknowledged the Porsche and poked his head through von Brockdorf's open window. He looked hard at Raven and Kirstie then opened the gate. The two cars moved into a complex of hangars and squat concrete buildings. Half-a-dozen passenger jets were drawn up on the wet tarmac. Blinking lights marked the runways. A fuel-tanker was linked to the Air France 727 standing in front of Terminal Two. Von Brockdorf stopped in front of a two storey edifice.

AIR FRANCE LUFTFEACHE   EINTRITT VERBOTEN!

A security-guard blocked the doorway. Raven could see more armed police positioned around the 727. Van Brockdorf turned.

"It won't be long now," he said to Kirstie.

She lifted her bag and cameras. "I never felt so important!"

It was bravely done but Raven knew the effort it took. She swung her long legs into the rain. Von Brockdorf led the way into a bare room with windows overlooking the wet waste of tarmac. Two men awaited them. One was an Air France ground-steward. The other wore the green uniform of the Frontier Police. A walkie-talkie buzzed on the crate between them. They spoke to the lawyer in German.

"They want your tickets and passports," he said.

Raven felt in his pocket, glancing away through the dirty window. The lights were on in the 727, passengers boarding the plane at both ends. The Air France employee spoke into the walkie-talkie. The Frontier guard touched the peak of his cap.

"Gute reise!"

Von Brockdorf's hand came out of his raincoat pocket. He gave the registered parcel to Raven. The seals had been broken. An envelope bearing the lawyer's office address was tucked under the twine. Von Brockdorf took Raven by the shoulders and looked hard into his eyes.

"This is as far as I go. I will call you tonight."

Raven nodded. The right words were difficult to find. Kirstie stepped in between them and kissed the lawyer on both cheeks. "You're a lovely man. Please come and see us in London."

Von Brockdorf's face reddened. "You may rely on it. Good-bye to you both."

Raven and Kirstie walked out to the waiting Porsche. They sat with their bags on their knees, uncomfortable in the cramped space behind. The Porsche took off, spraying water.

"You made that man blush," Raven accused.

She returned his look unabashed. "I wish I could do the same to you!"

A controlled skid brought the Porsche to a halt. The front end of the aircraft was closed but the steps at the back were still in position. A cabin-stewardess helped the Ravens aboard and into two empty seats at the rear. None of the other passengers seemed to have noticed their late arrival. NO SMOKING signs came on. The stewardess passed down the aisle, checking seatbelts. The 727 rose smoothly, and banked over the city and river. The rain and the mist were surmounted and the aircraft droned south. People started to move about. Cigarettes were produced.

Raven freed the envelope from the twine binding the parcel, anxious to get at the mock-leather diary inside. It fell open at Sunday March 30. The spaces were blank for the next five days. The entries started on Saturday April 5 and continued on Sunday 6 and Monday 7. The ink was green, the handwriting neat.

Raven unfolded the typewritten sheet and read the translation into English.

APRIL 5

11:45 P.M. Tea-dance at Montcalm Hotel. (Wore Miss Selfridge black dress and new shoes.) This man came over and asked me to dance! His name is Piers Pelham. He is English, thirty-four years old, and *very* sophisticated. He looks like a young Steve McQueen only his hair is white instead of blonde. He asked if he could join me and we started to talk. He is a property-dealer and has a house near the river in Putney. I'm impressed! He has travelled all over Europe. He took me to supper in Soho and we talked a lot more. It's the first time ever that I've met someone who really *understands*. He's divorced. He told me that his wife ran off with his best friend. His hair went white overnight! He drove me home to Hampstead and I'm seeing him tomorrow. Toi Toi Toi!!!

APRIL 6

11 P.M. Asked Mrs. W. if I could take the day off. She was *not* very pleased. Met Piers and went to his house in Putney. Utter bliss! It still seems incredible that someone with so much to offer would choose *me!* But *it's happened!* Gentle and kind and loving. I'm so happy! Piers has to see someone in Amsterdam and wants me to go with him. Got home quite late and told Mrs. W. that I intended to move in with Piers. She was

most disapproving. It was my life but she hoped that I knew what I was doing and so on. I simply do NOT CARE!
APRIL 7
I shall never make use of this diary again! I am sending it home. I want everything that was written before to be kept to remind me how hopeless life was before I met Piers. God has been very good to me.

He sat staring at the words, thoughts crashing like surf on an empty shore. He opened the envelope. The snapshot enclosed was of von Brockdorf's son, a facsimile of the one on the lawyer's desk. Raven read the letter.

Dear John,
Life's ironies are often hard to accept but I am certain that you are capable of doing so.
Remember that you have achieved your purpose! As a father I can count it a privilege to have met and in some degree to have known you.

Yours in friendship,
Helmut

Kirstie's voice came from a vast distance. He pulled himself together and gave her von Brockdorf's letter and the typewritten sheet.

She read them and shook her head. Her eyes were compassionate.

"Lauterbach's right," he said bitterly. "I only believe what I want to believe."

She tugged at his arm, forcing him to look at her. "Listen to me for once, *please!*" she said fiercely. "You did what you felt that you had to do and now it's all over. If it hadn't been for you those wretches would still be alive to go on spreading their misery. Think about that!"

"I do," he said. "But it isn't enough."

"Then what *is* enough?" she demanded. "The book? OK, write it. Anything rather than see you poison yourself like this!"

He put the diary and letter back in the brown-paper wrapping. "There isn't going to *be* any book, Kirstie. I'm going to call those people from the airport and cancel my appointment. You're right and I'm wrong. It's over and done with."

She pulled off her beret and shook her hair free. She gave him the freckle-nosed grin he would always remember.

"Know something, Raven? You're a lovely man, too. Don't ever change!"

He found himself smiling. In the higher reaches of his mind all was well.

About the Author

Donald MacKenzie is a well-known Canadian author who lives in Britain. There are thirteen titles featuring British Detective-Inspector John Raven which have been published here and abroad. A SAVAGE STATE OF GRACE is his fourth book for the Crime Club.